The Victory

Boys

Jamal Orme

THE ISLAMIC FOUNDATION

Published by
THE ISLAMIC FOUNDATION
Markfield Conference Centre, Ratby Lane, Markfield
Leicestershire, LE67 9SY, United Kingdom
E-mail: publications@islamic-foundation.com
Website: www.islamic-foundation.com

Quran House, P.O. BOX 30611, Nairobi, Kenya

P.M.B. 3193, Kano, Nigeria

Distributed by
KUBE PUBLISHING LTD
Tel +44 (01530) 249230, Fax +44 (01530) 249656
E-mail: info@kubepublishing.com
Website: www.kubepublishing.com

Author Jamal Orme
Editors Yosef Smyth and Fatima D'Oyen
Illustrator Eman Salem
Typesetter Nasir Cadir
Cover design Stan Ivanchev
Coordinator Anwar Cara

*A Cataloguing-in-Publication Data record for this book is available
from the British Library*

ISBN 978-0-86037-414-5 *paperback*

Printed by Imak Offset, Turkey

Dedication

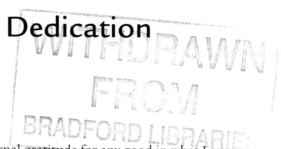

For God, eternal gratitude for any good in what I say;
And for my parents, who've encouraged me since Archimedes' day.

Contents

1. The Boys Hatch a Plan

'*Innahu kaana tawwabaa,*' chorused the children lazily.

Imam Munieb pushed his glasses to the top of his nose and scanned the room.

'Who can tell us the meaning of Surah *al-Nasr*,' he demanded.

A solitary hand shot into the air.

Mashallah, thought the Imam. You can always rely on Abdullah.

'Only Abdullah?' he growled.

All of the eyes in the room lowered. The children had the feeling that Imam Munieb was glaring directly at them, but not one of them dared to look up. It could be fatal.

'*Subhanallah!*' barked the Imam. 'This is one of the shortest, yet most important surahs in the whole of the Noble Qur'an! And once again, we must rely on clearly *the* most important student in the room to tell us its meaning!'

Abdullah straightened himself in his chair and cleared his throat.

'*Subhanallah,*' repeated Imam Munieb, with resignation in his voice. '*Tafadl, ya* Abdullah. Please tell us.'

'Well,' began Abdullah, who enjoyed any chance to demonstrate his knowledge, 'this is a Medinan surah, and its revelation was a clear sign to the Prophet – *sallallahu alayhi wa sallam* – that he was approaching the end of his life ... ' In the corner of the class at the madrasa, Ibrahim leaned towards his neighbour, Junayd.

'Did you see Match of the Day last night?' Ibrahim whispered.

'No, at the restaurant all night,' Junayd breathed back through gritted teeth.

' ... so,' Abdullah continued, 'when Allah *subhanahu wa ta'ala* says *"Fasabbih bihamdi rabbika wastaghfir"*, He is commanding the Prophet – *sallallahu alayhi wa sallam* – to praise Him and seek His forgiveness at this time, because all of the blessings are from Him and ... '

'Shame,' consoled Ibrahim. 'Great game at Anfield. Finished 3–3 in the end.'

'Who were they play ...'

'*Ibrahim! Junayd!*' yelled Imam Munieb. '*Why* are you talking?'

His eyes bore into them and both boys immediately looked down.

'Do you think,' he continued, 'you know all of this already?'

'No Imam,' answered Ibrahim quietly.

Junayd stayed focused on his feet and shook his head.

'Not one of you – not *any* of you can choose not to listen,' continued the Imam, an outstretched arm tracing a semi-circle of the room to include all 30 boys assembled, 'because this is your religion, your *deen*! And you have to know it!'

He took an exasperated breath, and carried on.

'Your *deen* is your protection, whether you know it or not! So *wake up*!'

There were only five minutes until break, and these were easily swallowed up by the remainder of Abdullah's explanation. Ibrahim and Junayd were soon on the small paved area in the mosque yard, idly leaning against a wall and complaining to one another.

'He doesn't have to go mental like that,' moaned Ibrahim, swishing long strands of black hair from his eyes. The mosque was only a hundred yards or so from the seafront and the wind always felt strong in the yard.

'I suppose we should have been listening,' said Junayd.

'What? To *Abdullah*? He's not my teacher.'

'He probably could be! He knows a lot more than I do anyway,' observed Junayd.

There was a short pause.

'I hate this,' said Ibrahim.

'What?'

'Madrasa. What's the point of it?'

'The Imam said it's to learn our religion ... ' began Junayd.

'That's what my Dad says,' interrupted Ibrahim, 'but I never see him doing the things we get told to do.'

'What do you mean?'

'I mean, I bet he doesn't know half of the stuff we get shoved down our throats every week. The only time he comes to the mosque is to drop me off for this stupid thing.'

'What about *jum'ah* prayers on Fridays?' asked Junayd.

'He prays it sometimes, but he's not bothered. He says you only have to go to one in three. I think he's got an alarm set on his phone so he doesn't miss three in a row.'

Junayd wasn't sure what to say. He decided to change the subject.

'You know what,' he said, 'it'd be good if we could play football in this break time.'

'Ha!' laughed Ibrahim. 'The Imam would *never* go along with that! He hates football! I heard him say it was one of the evils of modern society!'

'It turns brothers against brothers!' declared an exaggerated Libyan accent. It was Khalid. 'Isn't that what he said?'

'Yeah Khalid, he did say that,' said Ibrahim. 'But actually, think about it. The Imam never comes outside in the break. If we could get a football out here, he'd never know we were playing.'

'He'd hear all the noise,' warned Junayd.

'Not if we're quiet,' replied Ibrahim. 'Anyway, this was your idea!'

'It wasn't my idea to do it! I just said it would be good if we *could*!'

'Don't be a chicken,' scolded Khalid. 'I'll bring a ball next week and smuggle it out here before madrasa. Everyone stays calm – no danger. Got it?'

2. Silent Celebrations

The following week a nod and a smile from Khalid at madrasa was enough to tell Ibrahim and Junayd that the ball was in place outside. The eye contact around the classroom suggested that most of the boys knew of the plan for break time. There was an air of excitement and unexpected focus that morning.

Imam Munieb noticed the difference too. The children seemed happier and more hands went up for questions. Many of the answers were wrong but at least they had tried. *Alhamdulillah*, Imam Munieb thought: *with every hardship comes ease.*

As it drew near to break time, the Imam began to feel far more optimistic about helping these boys to know their religion.

Imam Munieb dismissed the class without a hint of his usual frustration and withdrew contentedly to the kitchen to make a cup of tea.

Once clear of the corridor, the boys raced down the steps to the yard. The delight of seeing Khalid's football against an outer wall drew squeals of joy from many of them!

'Football! Football!' chanted the more excited among them.

'Sssssshhhh!!' implored Khalid, thrusting a finger to his lips. 'Do you want the Imam to hear you? Think there'll be much "Football! Football!" if he finds out?'

Everyone was immediately quiet, but the smiles did not leave their faces.

'Right,' ordered Khalid, 'Ibrahim and I will pick the teams. No complaining, no noise. If you score, celebrate in silence. Anyone who makes too much noise will be booked, and then sent off.'

'Who's the referee?' ventured Abdullah, who was uncomfortable with doing something he knew Imam Munieb would disapprove of.

'I am,' said Khalid, defiantly.

'Why you? I thought you were playing?' Abdullah persisted. He was secretly hoping he could take on the role himself to avoid kicking the ball.

'Because it's *my* ball. Right, on my team, I'll have ... '

To everyone's glee and amazement, the game was a success. The two teams played out a three-all draw. All six goals were scored between the two sets of brick-stack posts that the boys had hastily assembled before kick-off from a pile of rubble in the corner of the yard.

Each goal had been celebrated with little more than a silent fist-pumping by the scorer – with the exception of the last two: Khalid's team mobbed little Faris when he poked in to make the score 3–2 with barely a minute left; and Ibrahim's last-second equaliser (or thereabouts) inspired him to pull off his jumper and swing it around his head as he raced around the yard in mute celebration. That was enough to draw laughter from all of the boys – even on Khalid's team.

Khalid was careful to end the match on time just in case the Imam heard the suspicious merriment. He took the ball and placed it in a circle of stones at the far end of the mosque wall, hidden.

'OK, sit down,' began Imam Munieb, and 30 tired boys collapsed into their seats. The Imam saw that their faces were shining with sweat and that quite a few among them were struggling to slow their breathing.

He was puzzled, though not suspicious.

'I think perhaps some of you worked too hard at break time,' he said. 'You are meant to work hard in madrasa, not in break time!'

It was meant to be a joke. But instead the boys were stirred into action, wiping their faces and sitting up straight as quickly as they could. Junayd began to wonder if he looked guilty and decided it was better to look at his feet. Then he remembered that looking at his feet was what he did when he *was* guilty. Not knowing where to look, he stared at Abdullah.

Abdullah was looking *extremely* guilty. Junayd wondered for a moment if Abdullah might confess the game to Imam Munieb. In the end he didn't say anything, so their secret was safe, at least until the following week.

***

Over the next couple of months the boys played football in their madrasa break. They showed remarkable self-restraint in their football sessions, largely because of Khalid's cautionary pre-match team talks, which were always delivered quickly (to maximise playing time) and with urgency (*'If we get caught, we can never play again!'*)

***

'You know, Fatimah,' Imam Munieb told his daughter one Sunday lunch after madrasa, 'I think those boys are really starting to learn something useful.'

'*Alhamdulillah, Baba,*' Fatimah replied.

Her sister Ruqayyah nodded her congratulations as she munched her cereal.

'*Mashallah,*' agreed their mother, Salamah. 'You don't just mean Abdullah then?'

Imam Munieb smiled.

'No, although he is still top of the class, *mashallah*! But you know, all of them are doing well. Most of them have memorised a part of the Qur'an in the last few weeks – can you imagine that? *Mashallah,*' he chuckled. 'To be honest with you, I did not look forward to madrasa a month ago. Now it is a pleasure for me.'

'*Alhamdulillah*,' said Salamah. 'You know, it is easier for me with the girls too – especially since Fatimah started to help me with the teaching.'

'Are you still working with the youngest children, *ya habibti*?' asked the Imam, turning to his eldest daughter.

'Yes *Baba*. I did some stories of the *sahabah* with them last week, just like you suggested. The younger ones really like that. I'm enjoying it, *alhamdulillah*.'

Ruqayyah smiled cheekily. 'She doesn't have a choice,' she joked. 'I'm not having my sister teach me!'

Fatimah gave her a playful nudge in the ribs and they both laughed.

'Ah yes,' said Imam Munieb, stretching his arms in relaxed contentment. 'We've been enjoying stories of the *sahabah* too. It's so much easier to cover subjects like that when the boys are keen, like they are now.'

He smiled peacefully.

'*Alhamdulillah*.'

He had no idea that the peace was about to shatter ...

3. Black Sheep

'Saleem!' came a voice from downstairs. '*Saleem*!'

Saleem sighed heavily.

'Yes, *Ubba*?'

'Saleem! Come downstairs now!'

Saleem trudged from his room and found his father glaring at him from the bottom of the staircase.

'What is it *Ubba*?'

'*Heshe kita khorray*?'

'I'm ... I'm not sure what I'm doing later. This and that.'

'You will help me in the restaurant from four o'clock.'

'I ... I can't, *Ubba*. I said I'd play football after college.'

'I need your help in the restaurant,' insisted his father. 'I'm not asking you. I'm telling you.'

'But *Ubba*, I told the guys ...'

'You told me you didn't know what you were doing!' interrupted his father. 'It's beginning to sound like the story of your life!'

Saleem threw him a resentful look and then quickly looked down at his feet.

'Don't look at me like that boy! You're eighteen years old and you're growing up to be a nobody! In Bangladesh eighteen makes you a man! Take a look at yourself, boy!

Your brother Junayd is more of a man than you and he's only twelve!'

Saleem was stung by his father's words.

'More of a man because he helps you in the restaurant, you mean?'

'*Kita khoss*?!' roared his father, bursting up the first few stairs. 'What did you say?!'

'Nothing,' mumbled Saleem.

'*Kita khoss*?!'

'Nothing!' he repeated angrily.

'Don't you raise your voice to me, boy!'

He paused, hunting furiously for the words with which to chastise his eldest son.

'You're bringing shame on this family, boy! Nobody in our family has ever been in trouble with the police before you! I'm ashamed of you! How can I tell your *dadi* about your behaviour? You're a disgrace to the family!

'And when I try to help you ... try to involve you in the family business, give you some grounding ... you throw it back in my face and go off to play football! You're not a man, you're a child! You're meant to set an example for your little brother ... what sort of an example are you, boy?'

'What sort of an example am *I*?' spat Saleem. 'What sort of an example are *you*?'

'*I beg your pardon*!' shouted his father, shaking with rage.

'I said what sort of an example are you? You're always coming out with this right and wrong stuff ... you're right, I'm wrong ... who *says* you're right, huh?'

'Who? *Who*? Allah in His Holy Qur'an tells us what is right and ...'

'Really?' interrupted Saleem. 'So what does Allah say about selling alcohol in your restaurant? And what did He say about missing your prayers so you can get ahead on chopping onions? I must have missed that bit in madrasa ...'

Before Saleem could finish his sentence, his father charged up the remainder of the stairs and made a grab for his son.

Saleem dived back and scurried into the bathroom. He slammed the door and slid the bolt into place.

'*O bydee ai*, you dog!' yelled his father, pounding the door with his fists. 'Come out now!'

Elsewhere in the house, Saleem's mother made a silent prayer for her family amidst the heart-trembling sound of banging and yelling.

In his room, Junayd crept nervously into his bed and pulled the covers over his head.

***

'So what did your brother do anyway?' asked Ibrahim, as curious as always.

'He was with some people who stole a car,' Junayd sighed. With the Imam's imminent arrival at madrasa, this was not the topic he wanted to discuss.

'He stole a car! No way!'

'No, he didn't steal it. He was just in it ...'

'Yeah well obviously he's not going to say he stole it, right!'

'He *didn't* steal it!'

'Alright, chill bro! So he didn't steal it. But he went to prison?'

'No, you weren't listening!' Junayd was beginning to get a little impatient. 'He got put in the cells. My dad had to go and collect him. He just got a warning, or something, because he didn't know the car was stolen.'

'I suppose,' admitted Ibrahim. 'If they thought he was involved he'd be going to court or something, right?'

'Whatever, I don't know,' sighed Junayd. His heart felt heavy whenever he thought about his brother. With all the tension between dad and Saleem, it was better to be anywhere but at home these days. In fact, Junayd realised suddenly and to his surprise, it was much better to be at madrasa.

'So, we're playing same teams as last week today?' Junayd asked, changing the subject.

'Yeah – it was a draw last week so we need to settle it, right?'

'We should have penalties if it's a draw again ...'

'That wouldn't be fair,' Ibrahim interrupted, 'your team's got Hasan. He's a wicked goalie. You'd win the shoot-out.'

'Exactly!' laughed Junayd.

An hour and a half of madrasa later and the boys were happily – and silently – involved in another epic game of yard football.

"With only a minute left on the clock, Faris and Adam linked up to give Khalid's team a 6–5 advantage.

Ibrahim, dispensing with usual caution, rallied his troops excitedly.

'Come on boys!' he yelled. 'We can't lose this!'

'Come on!' repeated his team-mates. 'Let's get this back! Let's get a goal!'

'Sshh,' attemped Khalid, but his opponents had already kicked off and were calling directions to one another.

'Man on!' Yunus warned Ismail, who promptly passed him the ball. Yunus sprayed it to the wing where Ali was in some space. Ali took a touch, and then slid an inch-perfect pass into the space ahead of Ibrahim, who was advancing on goal.

Ibrahim had anticipated it well, but so too had Khalid in defence. As the ball sped along the concrete, each player sensed that this was the final chance of the match. A good shot from Ibrahim would mean an equalising goal. A well-timed challenge from Khalid would mean victory for his team.

Just as Ibrahim was about to drive the ball goalwards, Khalid thrust a foot at the ball and smashed it clear ...

... *and* smashed the uppermost glass panel of the greenhouse in a neighbouring garden.

'*Oh no!*' came the collective cry.

Khalid dived for cover to avoid being seen. The others did the same, as if being fired upon by a greenhouse sniper.

All of the children on the ground made for a peculiar sight for Imam Munieb as he emerged into the yard.

4. A Change of Heart

'I do not have the words,' growled Imam Munieb to the boys, who had hastily and fearfully reassembled in the classroom expecting an explosion of anger from the Imam.

'It is dishonest,' he continued, his voice ever hinting at an escalation in volume, 'to sneak a ball into the mosque and to play with it without my permission. *And* you broke the window so you see how it is not sensible either!'

'But Imam, we only broke it today, we didn't ...' Ibrahim's voice trailed off as he realised what he was about to reveal.

'Didn't what?' demanded Imam Munieb.

'Er ...' Ibrahim blushed.

'Didn't what? Didn't do it before? You are telling me you have played *before*?'

Nobody said anything. He looked around.

'Is that what you're telling me?'

With no one volunteering an answer, he turned to a reliable source of information.

'Abdullah,' he said, his voice suddenly full of disappointment at the very thought that Abdullah could have been complicit. 'How long has this, this ... *football* ... been going on?'

'W-well,' stammered Abdullah, aware that all eyes were suddenly upon him, and for once unsure of his response, 'I think ... er ... a few weeks.'

'Tell me when it started Abdullah,' demanded the Imam, 'and I want the truthful and accurate answer.'

'Sunday, March the fourth, Imam.'

Incredulous that Abdullah should know the exact date and inform Imam Munieb, Ibrahim tutted.

Now came the explosion.

'*What did you make that sound for, Ibrahim*?!' roared Imam Munieb, his cheeks visibly reddening above his thick black beard. 'You think you have the most right to that sound? I think right now I have the most right to it! I ask you and I ask you truthfully, are *you* behind this? Is this *your* idea, Ibrahim?!'

Ibrahim was somewhat cheeky, but equally he was honest.

'Yes, Imam,' he said.

'And it was your ball too, I suppose!'

This time Ibrahim said nothing.

'It was my ball,' murmured Khalid.

'Your ball, Khalid!' said Imam Munieb. 'You are together in this?'

'Yes, Imam,' admitted Khalid.

'Well at least you have *some* honesty! But not much, because there is no honesty in doing something when you know that if you ask me first I will say no!'

'We just wanted ...' began Ibrahim.

'What do you *just want* now, Ibrahim?' cried the Imam. 'After all is said and done and after the damage you have caused, what is it that you *just want*?'

'Nothing,' replied Ibrahim.

'No, I think you should tell us! I think if there is something that makes you do something like this ... makes *all of you* do something like this ... we need to know what it is that you *just want*!'

Ibrahim squeezed his hands together anxiously.

'Tell me, Ibrahim!'

'We just wanted to have some fun,' he said.

The following Sunday, madrasa was subdued. No one had dared to bring in a ball, and in any case, the Imam had arranged for Fatimah to bring his cup of tea to him outside during the break. He perched uncomfortably on one of the stone steps and glared at the boys occasionally as a reminder.

At the end of the session, Imam Munieb announced that there were some letters to take home for parents to 'treat as urgent'.

'These are to tell your parents about the damage you caused last week,' he explained bitterly. 'The damage has been repaired but the cost of repair will be paid for by you. Since you were *all* involved, you share the punishment. The letter tells you how much money you must bring, *in cash*, by next Sunday. *Do not* go home and ask your parents for this money. Do jobs for people to earn it. And you must bring the money next Sunday.'

Ibrahim gazed up at the ceiling and started thinking of reasons why he wouldn't be bringing the money in a week. Imam Munieb saw him and read his mind.

'Do not give me excuses because Mr and Mrs Bateman from Number 18, whose window you smashed, will be coming to the mosque on that day to accept the money from you and to give you a chance to apologise. If you do not bring the money you owe them, I will point out to them which of you did not honour your responsibility. If you learn from your mistakes you will become better Muslims.'

The last thing Junayd intended to do was to pass the letter to his father. Junayd was scared that his father would blame it on his brother's bad example.

'Saleem,' he whispered the following day at home, 'Can you think how I can raise five pounds?'

'Eh?' grunted Saleem, crashing onto the sofa next to his brother. 'What do you need five pounds for?'

'We broke a window at the mosque.'

'Ha! Those madrasa sessions must be getting livelier than when I used to go!'

'Very funny,' replied Junayd, unmoved. 'We have to pay for the repair.'

'Tell you what,' suggested Saleem, 'you get *Ubba* off my back and I'll give you the five pounds myself.'

'How would I do that?' asked Junayd.

'I don't know. Next time he tries to force me to work at the restaurant, jump in and offer to do it yourself. Make out you *really* want to.'

'OK!' agreed Junayd. 'That's fair enough.'

'There's nothing fair about it little bruv. He should be paying you more than a fiver for what you do for him. But anyway, I'll stump up the dough if you do that for me.'

Junayd wondered if Saleem even had five pounds, but he was happy enough to go along with the idea. After all, it might make things a bit easier at home.

'How did you break a window anyway?'

'Football. Khalid kicked the ball and it hit a greenhouse at Number 18.'

'You guys are allowed to play football now?' said Saleem, impressed. 'Wicked!'

'Er, no,' replied Junayd.

'Oh. I see. Bet the Imam's chuffed,' said Saleem. 'Hey, I know how you can raise the five pounds another way then.'

'How's that?' asked Junayd.

'Life insurance,' replied his brother. 'If you don't pay up for the damages, I'd say there's a pretty good chance the Imam will kill you next week. Your life must be worth at least a fiver.'

One way or another the boys raised the money for Mr and Mrs Bateman the following week. Khalid had grudgingly washed his dad's car. Accepting that there was no way around the punishment, Ibrahim had wanted to cut his little brother's hair, but his mum would only trust him with the garden hedge. And, of course, Junayd had put in an extra couple of shifts at the restaurant, for which Saleem had honoured his pledge of a fiver. Junayd had showed such enthusiasm that he wasn't sure whether he was being paid for his chopping, peeling and washing up; or for his acting skills.

The Batemans were quite understanding and forgiving. A little too much so, thought Imam Munieb.

'I remember what it was like to be your age,' said Mr Bateman. 'It's a shame that yard's so small, too. You could do with a bigger spot for a good game of football.'

'Yes, but of course the mosque is not a place for football,' interjected the Imam. 'I am trying to explain this to the boys so they learn to be more responsible and to see how their actions can affect other people.'

'Oh, don't you worry,' replied Mr Bateman unhelpfully. 'They're a good bunch of lads, this lot. They just need to learn to shoot straight.'

After that, madrasa sessions reverted to their more familiar and established form. The boys yawned their way through them, only chancing the occasional hushed conversation when they thought they could get away with it. Enthusiasm for learning the Qur'an dwindled, as did any willingness to ask questions. Or to see the relevance of madrasa to their lives in a twenty-first century seaside town. Once more Imam Munieb began to find little pleasure in the sessions; except in the hope of his rewards for delivering them.

***

'These boys, nothing touches them,' Imam Munieb complained to his wife, over dinner, one evening. 'I can talk and talk, but they don't hear me. Or if they do, I don't think it touches their hearts.'

Salamah tried to console him.

'It's the same with the girls, you know,' she said. 'So many people don't feel the beauty of Islam. It's not the children's fault – they're only picking up on the messages they're getting. Even the Sunday madrasa is part of that – once a week the doors swing open, the children tramp in – over to you, sister.'

'It's true,' agreed the Imam. 'Two weeks ago, one of the fathers came to me. He demanded to know how the boys could break a window when they're coming to the mosque to learn their Islam. I said "I am glad you realise how much we need the parents to help with the madrasa, to supervise all of the children."'

'Did he come last week? What do you think?'

Salamah smiled sympathetically.

'Do they think that Islam is a part-time course?' Imam Munieb sighed deeply. '*Ya habibti* ... we need these parents to take the matter seriously!'

He looked at his wife, hoping she might offer a solution.

'It's a test,' she said. 'A test for all of us.'

'I have been trying,' said Imam Munieb, shaking his head. 'Perhaps I've been trying the wrong things.

Imam Munieb's mind was a whirl of problems and dead-ends. He prayed to Allah to renew his patience, to keep him steadfast, and to show him how he might genuinely improve the situation for his community.

A few days later, the Imam had an idea that went against all of his instincts – an idea that he could not quite believe he was seriously considering. He prayed for Allah's guidance and resolved to give it a try, if Allah would so will it.

Imam Munieb was going to start a football team.

5. 'Imam Munieb's Going to Start a What?!'

There was only one problem for Imam Munieb: he didn't really know a great deal about the game.

All he knew about football was that it made people hostile to one another and it was a distraction from living a righteous life.

Still, he had made the intention. His intention was to bring the boys together in a way they would enjoy, and to take the chance to teach them more of their religion when opportunities arose. He had also dared to dream that it might attract help from the community. Suddenly it became of paramount importance for him to get at least one parent to help him run the team – or, even better, to take over the whole thing. At present, he couldn't think of anybody who might be interested.

Naturally, he had no plans to abandon the madrasa. He thought better of allowing any football to take place in the yard. One smashed greenhouse was already one too many. And, he thought, what impression would it give to the neighbours if he was seen to endorse the football games in the yard after that little disaster?

So, on the very next Sunday, and after a touch of literary assistance from Fatimah, Imam Munieb handed out thirty letters to a set of open-mouthed, incredulous Muslim boys. Not one of them could believe their eyes.

After the lesson, when it had sunk in, each of them rushed to their parents in unbridled excitement.

'*Listen to this! Imam Munieb's going to start a football club*!'

'What are you talking about, Yunus?'

'Don't be silly, Faris!'

'*What* did you say, Ali?'

'Imam Munieb's going to start a *what*?!'

'Listen! I'll read you the letter myself!'

Dear Brothers and Sisters in Islam,

As-salamu 'alaykum wa rahmatullahi wa barakatuh.

Beginning next Sunday, *inshallah*, the boys' madrasa will finish at 11.30am rather than midday.

From 11.30am until 12.30pm there will be football for the boys, which will take place in Radwell Gardens. *Inshallah* it is hoped the boys will eventually be able to play some matches, and that this project will be beneficial for their development as young Muslims.

This is an ambitious project and I will need assistance from the community. Please come to see me next week, or at a suitable time, to declare your interest.

Your brother,
Imam Munieb Mahmood

'He's crazy,' exclaimed Yunus' father.

'You've got to be joking,' said Faris' dad.

'*What* did you say, Ali?'

***

Imam Munieb had not expected any support with the football club; nor had he prepared a *Plan B* were he to find himself working solo. So when Adam's father marched through the mosque door the following Sunday morning, he was delighted to think that his brother might wish to lend a hand. Even if it proved to be a case of 'the blind leading the blind'.

'*As-salamu alaykum*, Brother Munieb,' he began.

'*Wa 'alaykum as-salam wa rahmatullah*,' came the reply.

'I would like to talk to you about the football team,' continued Adam's father.

'Yes, please do.'

'Are you mad?' he asked, straight-faced.

'Excuse me?'

'The mosque pays you to be our spiritual leader, to lead our prayers and to teach our children. Now you want to run a football club?'

Imam Munieb chose his words carefully.

'Brother, I am still doing all of those things you say. I hope that the football club ... '

'But,' interrupted Adam's father, 'you are taking the time from the madrasa to give to the football club. That is thirty minutes less time for learning. How can you justify this in the House of Allah?'

'Brother,' insisted Imam Munieb as calmly as he could, 'you may not be aware of this, but the children have a half-hour break. From today there will not be ... '

'Yes, and what do they do with their break? Smash windows! And how do you reward them? By letting them play *more* football, so they can smash *more* windows!'

'I remind you that there will be the same amount of teaching time for your son. I have learned from what you have said that you have not come to give your help, which would have been welcome. If you do not want Adam to play football, please collect him at 11.30am. *As-salamu alaykum.*'

Adam's father stood and mouthed a few silent words in disbelief. He then turned on his heels and marched outside.

There were no other adult visitors that morning, and certainly no offers of help. However, it was noticeable once again to Imam Munieb how much more receptive the boys were during madrasa. He reflected ruefully that the impact of football was almost like flicking a switch:

Football = focus;

No football = no interest.

What a shame, thought the Imam, that these boys should need football to love learning Islam. Yet perhaps that was just part of the equation in this time and in this place, whether he liked it or not. *Inshallah*, a love of the *deen,* their religion, could grow out of anything, and all guidance is from Allah *subhanahu wa ta'ala.*

A short while later, the Imam found himself in unfamiliar territory: a large patch of grass. There were 28 boys aged 10 to 15 staring at him ... and one football.

'OK, we need two teams,' he began, still not quite sure of what he was embarking upon.

'Only one ball?' asked Ibrahim. 'There's a lot of us here ...'

'Where are the goals?' asked Ali, a puzzled look on his round, moonlike face.

The Imam looked around. It was quite true: there were no goals.

'Give me your jumper,' Khalid said to Yunus, who did as he was told and promptly began to shiver in the coastal breeze.

'And yours,' he added, pointing at Faris.

'I'll be cold,' replied Faris, trying his best to be assertive in spite of his diminutive frame.

'You'll be even colder if you have to stand around here waiting for me to find enough jumpers for goalposts. Now give it.'

Imam Munieb spoke. 'It is better for you, Khalid, if you speak the good words. Like please, *Min fadlik,* and thank you, *Shukran jazeelan,* Khalid.'

'Yes Imam,' nodded Khalid. Faris and the other boys sniggered.

'And Faris,' said the Imam.

'Yes Imam?'

'It is better for *us* if you give Khalid your jumper, please. *Now.* Thank you.'

As one might expect, a game of fourteen-a-side was never going to be straightforward. Occasionally the boys' frustration led them to ask Imam Munieb questions that seemed, to him, quite incomprehensible.

'*Imam, why don't we have rolling subs? There's too many of us on the pitch!*'

'*Imam, Hasan's got to go home. Can we have rush goalie?*'

'*Imam, are we playing offsides?*'

'*Play on!*' cried the Imam on each occasion, which the boys interpreted as meaning 'no', and as a signal not to ask again. Out of respect, they did not.

'Isn't that your brother?' Ibrahim asked Junayd as a hooded youth ambled towards them.

Junayd looked up.

'Oh yeah, that's Saleem. I think my dad must have forced him to come and get me.'

Saleem drew closer and looked on with interest. His presence encouraged Junayd to perform with a renewed purpose, and he darted around the pitch in pursuit of the ball.

'Good tackle bruv!' called Saleem approvingly. 'Give it to the winger!'

Junayd passed the ball wide as instructed, and Ali took it on his instep.

'*Skin him!*' shouted Saleem to Ali, asking him to beat his opponent for pace. Ali did so, but then found himself isolated in the corner of the pitch.

'*Give him an option!*' yelled Saleem this time.

For Imam Munieb, this dizzying array of new words had not passed unnoticed. *Winger*, *skin*, giving an *option* ... not to mention *rolling goalies* and *rush subs*, or whatever it was he'd heard. Clearly he had much to learn if he was going to make any sense of this game.

In the meantime, however, he dared to conclude that this first football session had been a success: a good turnout, enjoyment by all (including, he realised, himself), and ... best of all ...

... *No* smashed windows.

6. The Plot Slickens

'Hello, is Ibrahim there please?'

'Who's calling?'

'Junayd.'

'*As-salamu 'alaykum Junayd*, how are you?'

'Fine. Er, fine thank you, Mrs. Khan. Er, *wa 'alaykum as-salam*.'

'OK, just a minute Junayd, I'll call him.'

'Junayd?'

'Hey! Listen, there's going to be a football tournament in three weeks' time. We've got to tell the Imam so we can have a team and it's six-a-side but it's for under-thirteens so we can be in it but some of the boys won't be able ...'

'Stop, stop! What are you talking about? A football tournament? Where? Are you sure? Who told you about it?'

Junayd took a deep breath and attempted to explain his plan more clearly.

'A boy called Jake at my school told me. He plays for a team. I think they're called Sedgecombe Shuttles or something like that. They won their league last year, he said, and he scored forty-eight goals.

'Anyway, it's in three weeks, on a Sunday I think, I don't know where but it must be near here if Jake's playing, but anyway we've got to tell the Imam and make him take us there ...'

'Junayd!! Stop talking!' begged Ibrahim. 'You're giving me a headache, man!'

For a moment, all he could hear was Junayd's quick breathing.

'Right, thank you. Now,' said Ibrahim, 'there are a few things we need to sort out if this is going to happen. Firstly, you said it might be a Sunday. That's a madrasa day and I'm not sure the Imam will like the idea of playing in the morning because that would be *instead of* madrasa.'

'Hmm,' pondered Junayd.

'Secondly,' continued Ibrahim, 'I don't know much about football tournaments, but do you think they're going to let us turn up on the day and take part?'

'Hmm, well ...' began Junayd.

'Well of course they're not,' Ibrahim went on. 'We need to know exactly where and when it's happening. That's if your friend is right about there even being a tournament. We need to find out if we have to pay, what we're going to need, and all that stuff. And more important than that – are there any spaces for extra teams.'

'Hmmm ...'

'And we're going to need to do that very quickly, because I don't think the Imam will say yes unless we get all of the information for him. We've only had one week of football with him and he gave a penalty against Hasan for handball. OK, so at least he knew what handball is, but Hasan's the *goalkeeper*, you see what I'm saying?'

'Hmmm...'

'Seriously, I think the Imam's going to say no unless we make it real easy for him.'

'Hmmm ...'

'So, let's get some tasks sorted out. Unfortunately since you're the only one who knows this Jack ...'

'Jake.'

'Whatever ... you're the one who's going to need to do all the homework on this. You've got until tomorrow to get all the details. In the meantime I'll think about how to persuade the Imam to let us do it.'

'I ... tomorrow ... why tomorrow?'

'My dad says people work better under pressure.'

'Hmmm ... I don't ...'

'What have you got to worry about? I've given myself the difficult job! I'm going to need to learn hypnosis before I talk to the Imam.'

***

'*Ya* Allah,' she said, hands spread and head bowed. '*Ya* Allah, You alone do we worship and from You alone do we seek help. *Ya* Allah, there is no barrier between You and the prayer of the parent for their child. *Ya* Allah, please guide my son and make him a better Muslim, and *Ya* Allah, forgive us for failing him ...'

'*Ho qutah!*' came an angry voice from the next room. 'Where is the lazy dog now? *Shunna?* Where is Saleem?'

A tear slid down her cheek and landed in her open palm.

'*Shunna?!*'

'I don't know,' she sniffed.

***

A bright Thursday morning found the sunlight streaming in through Imam Munieb's tiny office window and illuminating the paper upon which he was making notes for the week's *khutbah,* the sermon he gave each Friday. He had chosen for its topic the importance of raising one's children well. It was a subject he revisited frequently, and not because of its success; he sometimes had the feeling that the majority of his congregation did not listen to his sermons. Especially those who arrived just as he was finishing.

A spare moment was a rare occasion for the Imam because there was always something that needed doing in the mosque. It was in disrepair, having been built nearly two hundred years ago as a school. It had not aged well. Walls crumbled, pipes rusted and the boiler was prone to inaction when it was most needed. Fortunately, Imam Munieb was blessed with a practical mind and skilful hands, and could fix most of these problems by himself.

Of course there were also the classes for adults the Imam held on Qur'an recitation, the meaning of the Qur'an, and the Arabic language. These were poorly attended, and often those who did stay for such a class would do so for a few weeks and then disappear once more.

As a result, the Imam remained in his own company around the mosque, or with Salamah and their teenaged daughters in their small apartment on its top floor, which had originally been built for a single caretaker.

As he meditated on the sermon he was writing, he became vaguely aware of a knocking on the side door of the apartment. This door was accessible from the sisters' prayer room and he heard Salamah's footsteps trail off in its direction followed by the creak of an opening door.

'*As-salamu 'alaykum,*' came a fragile, jumpy voice.

'*Wa 'alaykum as-salam,*' replied his wife, with a concerned tone. 'Please, come in. Are you alright?'

'*Alhamdulillah*,' said the woman. 'But, oh sister, I have terrible, big worry. My son ...'

Imam Munieb heard the voice descend into sobs, large jolting ones that his wife now tried to relieve with soft, consoling words.

He decided he should respect their privacy and tiptoed out of the room, into the narrow hallway, and out of the front door into the mosque.

'I ... just ... don't know ...' he heard the sobs continue, though less audible now. 'Saleem! I ... just ... don't know ... what to do!'

7. An Unexpected Offer

'You know the problem with children these days,' explained Mr Bateman, holding a wet paintbrush in his hand and waving it for emphasis, 'they're too old.'

'Forgive me, I do not understand,' replied Imam Munieb with a bemused smile. He folded his arms and patiently waited for his neighbour to explain. Mr Bateman, who looked somewhat unstable standing at the top of a ladder, took a break from repainting his garage wall and sat at the edge of its roof.

'Yes, it sounds strange doesn't it,' he chuckled. 'What I mean to say is, a child should stop being a child when he or she comes of age, if you get my meaning?'

'Yes, I know what you are saying,' nodded the Imam.

'But these days, they get to sixteen, eighteen ... twenty, even, and what can they do?'

He paused.

'I mean, what can they actually do?'

'Well, I ...'

'I mean when I was sixteen,' continued Mr Bateman, the paint now dripping from his brush onto the foot of his ladder, 'I knew how to fix a car, I even knew how to shear a sheep. I grew up around here of course. Back then we had farms, we had real, manual work to do – but, these kids, what can they do? Read and write ... that's about the sum of it. And not all of them can do that, can they?'

'Yes, I know, but education is very impor ...'

'Education's a red herring, my friend,' interrupted his neighbour. 'I mean no offence, but what I'm saying is that if you put these so-called educated children in a real life situation ... well, you're a praying man, aren't you? So maybe you can pray for them, because God knows they'll need all the help they can get.'

Imam Munieb felt that he should have had more to say in response to Mr Bateman because he firmly believed in the importance of a good education. To him it was simple: a good education led to a discerning mind, and a discerning mind was better equipped to recognise The Truth – The Truth of The Creator. But it was hard to argue with him after overhearing his wife's visitor earlier in the day.

He knew Saleem from when he had attended madrasa a few years back and, he recalled ruefully, he had never been the easiest to teach. *There* was a boy, thought the Imam, whose armour had been pierced because of a weakness in his religion, and who didn't seem at all sure who he was or what he wanted to be.

And yes, perhaps Mr Bateman's theory had some validity when applied to Saleem. He'd been all the way through secondary school and had now enrolled – albeit reluctantly – in college. Yet, from what Salamah had relayed, he was having significant differences with his father and had even been in trouble with the police. It didn't bode well.

***

The following Sunday there was an outbreak of fever among the boys at madrasa.

Football fever.

Word had reached Khalid that a possible tournament was in the offing for the football team. And whenever Khalid decided something was worth publicising, he set about the task with gusto.

'Everyone behave yourselves today!' he ordered, before the Imam had entered the room. 'We're going to ask the Imam about playing in a football tournament in two weeks. Don't give him a reason to say no, everyone got that?'

Suddenly the room was humming with excited chatter, as those not yet 'in the know' hunted down the finer details from others, many of whom knew no better than they did. Speculation turned to fact, so much so that small pockets of the classroom were prepared to believe anything: from the award of big prize money for the tournament winners, to the visit of scouts from the top football clubs, and the attendance of international superstars to present the medals (made of real gold and silver, naturally).

Imam Munieb was delighted to observe a real return to form during the morning madrasa; he had never heard the boys recite Qur'an this well, with so few mistakes all round. There were also plenty of suggestions regarding the meanings of the part of the Qur'an they were reading. In addition, he realised towards the end of the session, not once had he found himself admonishing a boy for idle chatter or fooling around.

Alhamdulillah, he whispered repeatedly.

When they arrived at Radwell Gardens, Imam Munieb delegated the tasks of organising the pitch and the teams to

Khalid, who was clearly assertive and charismatic enough to get the job done quickly. Sure enough, within a few minutes 22 of the boys were eagerly racing around the pitch in good-natured competition.

Imam Munieb was puzzled to see six boys standing on the side, chatting to one another.

'What are you doing, boys? The game has started!'

'We're rolling subs, Imam,' replied Yunus, his shaggy dark hair whipped up by the wind.

'You're rolling what?' queried the Imam. 'I don't see you rolling anything.'

'Rolling subs,' repeated Yunus, stifling a snigger. 'Rolling substitutes. It means when someone comes off the pitch, we take their place ...'

' ... But they can go back on again later,' added Abdullah, who had already begun to apply his usual zeal to mastering a new subject (and, truth be told, was keener to take on some sort of official role than to play).

The Imam nodded thoughtfully.

'I see,' he said. 'But I think you will get cold standing here doing nothing. Run around the pitch. Three laps.'

'What?' protested Yunus, before remembering what Khalid had said earlier. He quickly did as he had been told.

'*Backpass!*' came a chorus of voices near one of the goals. Imam Munieb whirled around to see Hasan clutching the ball uncertainly and several boys holding up their hands in expectant appeal.

Backpass? thought Imam Munieb. What is this *backpass* they're yelling about?

'*Play on!*' he shouted.

At around quarter past twelve, Imam Munieb saw the approach of a figure, and of an opportunity. It was Saleem.

'Come on Junayd! Get into space to receive it!' he called, as the Imam drew up beside him.

'*As-salamu 'alaykum* Brother Saleem,' he said softly, offering his hand.

Saleem turned his head, surprised not to have noticed the Imam, and shook his hand.

'*Wa 'alaykum as-salam*, Imam.'

'You know a lot about the game of football, I think.'

'Er, yeah. Quite a lot. I've always played football. Great game.'

'Not my sport, I must say,' admitted Imam Munieb. 'I like table tennis. Yes, I prefer table tennis, or a game of chess.'

'That's not even a ...' began Saleem. 'I mean, it's not really a sport, is it? Chess?'

'It's a sport for the mind, Saleem,' said Imam Munieb. 'And I must tell you, I find it easier to play than I find football to understand! What is a *backpass*?'

'Oh, ha, right,' laughed Saleem. 'It's when someone kicks the ball back to their own goalkeeper. He's not allowed to pick it up.'

'It would be a handball?'

'Er, no, it wouldn't be handball, it's just ... it's a rule. It makes it more interesting.'

'More interesting,' considered the Imam doubtfully. 'Hmmm.'

'So,' said Saleem, 'if you don't mind me asking ... why are you running a football club if you don't like ... *or know* about it?'

'Ah, Saleem,' he replied, a broad smile forming on his lips, 'a very good question.'

'*Penalty*!' cried Ibrahim, sprawled on the turf, part buried under Ismail's sizeable frame.

'Did you see that?' twitched the corner of Imam Munieb's mouth. 'Was it a penalty?'

'He fell over,' said Saleem. 'No penalty.'

'*Play on!*' called the Imam, to a chorus of groans.

'I started the club,' he explained, 'because I think these boys need a good, halal way of being with one another. I think they love football and I think they need a good, positive relationship with each other and with Islam – they are all Muslims, after all. So I think we need the club and *inshallah* I can help them to learn their religion through the madrasa *and* through the football. Most of my life I have studied – studied Islam, I mean – so I know little about the football, but I am here for those life lessons, which come in all parts of someone's life, not just when they are in a classroom. Does that make sense?'

Saleem had been listening carefully. He nodded, impressed.

'Yes, that sounds like a great idea,' he said.

'I was hoping you would say that,' replied Imam Munieb. 'Why?'

'Because I am going to ask *you* to run the club.'

'*What?*' exclaimed Saleem. 'I mean, sorry Imam, why? Why me?'

'I think you will be good for these boys, Saleem,' insisted the Imam.

'*Me?*' said Saleem disbelievingly. 'I don't think so ... I mean, do you really think their parents would want *me* to run the club instead of y ...'

'Saleem,' interrupted Imam Munieb. 'Every one of us has difficulties. We have tests from Allah *subhanahu wa ta'ala*. But Allah gives us opportunities as well, and He follows hardship with ease. I see a young man with an opportunity. I see him helping his younger brothers with a sport he likes and knows very much about. I see him finding out that, actually, he has a lot to offer them – and himself. A lot more than he realises at this moment.

'Wouldn't *you* call that an opportunity, Saleem?'

Imam Munieb clapped his hands three times to announce the end of training.

'*Mashallah*, a very good game today boys,' he enthused. 'Shake hands with each other, give salams.'

This was done with minimum fuss, and almost immediately Imam Munieb found himself encircled by 28 boys with hopeful expressions.

Imam Munieb was suspicious.

'What? What is it?'

'Imam,' began Ibrahim cautiously. 'As you know, we all love your football club, and we're very grateful for the time you have spared for us ...'

A compliment. Imam Munieb's suspicion grew.

' ... we've worked really hard in madrasa and we've all agreed that if we had to we would all come to madrasa on a different day, like Saturday, if there was something happening on Sunday ...'

They're definitely up to something, thought Imam Munieb.

' ... and there's a football tournament in two weeks – under-thirteen's only ...'

'*Oh!*' groaned the handful of 14 and 15 year-olds. 'You didn't tell us *that*!'

' ... at Hilsham School,' Ibrahim continued, 'and there *are* spaces left for teams to enter and we *do* have enough players for a team and we *can* pay for our entry and all wear the same colour and we can do madrasa on Saturday instead because it's a ten o'clock start on the Sunday if that's OK with ...'

'Enough!' cried Imam Munieb. 'Yes, we will enter.'

'Oh *please* Imam!' begged Khalid. 'We'll work really hard and we'll behave ourselv ... what did you say?'

'He said yes!' exclaimed Junayd. 'He said *yes*!'

There was a cacophony of shouts, screams and squeals as the boys jumped up and down in unison, punching the air and hugging one another as if they had won the tournament already.

'Shush, shush, *quiet*!' insisted Imam Munieb, sliding an arm around Saleem as he did so. 'I have an announcement to make,' he continued.

'Allow me to introduce your new football coach.'

8. Taking Charge

With only a single Sunday left before the tournament itself, Junayd knew that he had only one opportunity to impress his brother and secure a place in the team.

The chances of doing so appeared to have improved considerably when Saleem informed him one evening that he had just returned from a meeting with the Imam, who had told him that they would be entering *two* teams into the competition.

'That's two squads of eight, I reckon,' said Saleem with an unusual air of enthusiasm.

'*You* had a meeting with the Imam?' checked Junayd, doubtfully.

'S'wot I said isn't it? He told me I'm in charge but he'll be there for any support I might need. Plus he told me there'd be some moolah available for a few essentials ...'

'What are you going to spend that on? What *essentials*?' probed Junayd.

'Never you mind bruv,' replied Saleem, raising an eyebrow. 'I'm the coach here. You need to spend more time thinking about how you're going to win a place in my team!'

The next session, Saleem cut an assertive figure and seemed to have the immediate respect of all of the boys – or at the very least they appeared a little wary of him. Junayd wasn't entirely sure whether this was due to his age, or the fact that everyone knew he'd been recently arrested.

'Now listen up guys,' he began, every pair of eyes fixed on his. 'By the end of today I need to know who our best two squads of eight are. We'll be going for an 'A' and a 'B' because we wanna win it, so the 'A's gonna carry our main weaponry. 'B's won't be a pushover neither from what I've seen so far. It's up to you guys today to show me who should be in each squad. And,' he cautioned, 'you're not all gonna make it. No tears at the end, or else.'

Junayd noticed Imam Munieb standing some way to the side of his brother – leaving the platform to his new coach, as if to demonstrate his confidence in him.

'Now,' continued Saleem, 'not wanting to confuse you, but I'm gonna be switching things round a little bit as we go. We're gonna have four teams of seven, but you might find yourself being put on another team at short notice, so be flexible.'

'How are we going to have four teams?' asked Ibrahim. 'We've only got one ball.'

'All taken care of, bro,' replied Saleem, plopping three bright yellow balls out of a large nylon bag.

'Right, let's have a quick warm-up.'

None of the boys could claim to have exerted themselves more in a sport than they did that day. When Saleem blew the whistle at twenty-five past twelve, they collapsed on to the ground and lay there, unspeaking, their bellies heaving up and down desperately; their gasping was the only sound to be heard.

'Good session guys,' said Saleem. 'Here's the news you've been waiting for. No questions until I've finished. No arguments. If you're not where you wanted to be, accept it with some style, OK?'

'None of you has faith,' added Imam Munieb, speaking for the first time in the whole session, 'until he wants for his brother what he wants for himself.'

Saleem nodded approvingly. He did not remember hearing this saying before and found a certain beauty in it.

'OK, here we go. 'A' team. The goalie is Hasan. Defenders will start as Khalid and Yunus. Midfielders are Ali and Junayd. Ibrahim you're the striker. Captain is Khalid. Subs are Ismail and Faris. Everyone got it? Be at Hilsham by 9.30 in the morning or your place goes to a 'B' teamer. That's not a threat, it's a promise. Anyone got a problem?'

He looked around for any signs of dissent. He found none.

'Right, 'B' team ...'

Junayd could not help but be impressed by the conduct of his brother since becoming the coach. Not only did he make a seriously charismatic leader (perhaps even more so than Khalid, who was, everyone accepted, the natural choice as captain) but he also seemed to have become extremely well organised.

The latest evidence of this was when, with a little help from Junayd, Saleem phoned around the 'A' and 'B' team members to inform them that there would be extra training straight after the one-off Saturday madrasa.

'We need to work on a few things,' he explained to Junayd after they had made the calls. 'It's mainly the 'A' team I'm working with, but you can't practise against thin air. Give those 'B's a footballing lesson and remind me why I picked you ahead of them in the first place.'

'Football,' Saleem told them at the training session on Saturday before the 'A' team triumphed 8–2, 'is not a difficult game. Every time you pass, you move into an empty space so you can get the ball back. If the other team have got the ball, you make sure you're where you're meant to be – back in position. Got it?'

Unbeknown to all of the boys except Junayd, Saleem had sat down for a couple of chats with Imam Munieb and had begun to see his life a little differently. He wouldn't dare admit it to anyone, but he felt there was a great virtue in coaching these boys; using what he knew to do something for those who could benefit from it.

In addition, the Imam had set him two challenges, both of which he was trying very hard to keep to.

Firstly: to not swear.

'You are an example to these boys,' the Imam had said to him, the words sounding at first disapproving and familiar. 'So please, set them the *good* example. That includes speaking only the good, and saying nothing if there is nothing good to say.'

Secondly: to look at his own character and not the faults of others.

'When you feel things depend upon you,' Imam Munieb had told him, 'you are even more likely to be upset with the ones who make things difficult for you. You may be quick to criticise them. You must stop yourself, and look at the action. Look at it and ask yourself, "Do I do this? Can I criticise when I am just the same?" You are here to show these boys the right way, but try to better yourself as well.'

These advices had lodged in Saleem's heart; once again he had perceived a great beauty in them.

He was watching the boys train on Saturday when he suddenly realised why they struck a chord with him: They were two advices he wished would reach his father.

9. The Victory Boys

The big day had arrived!

Recalling Saleem's 'promise', all of the 'A' team members had assembled outside the gates of Hilsham Secondary School before they had even opened to the public. In fact, it was Saleem and Junayd who were the last to arrive, albeit with fifteen minutes still to spare until the deadline.

'Where's Imam Munieb?' asked Ibrahim. 'He's going to come, isn't he?'

'He'll be here bro,' Saleem assured him. 'Now then guys, take a look at *these*!'

Saleem lay down a rather large bag and unzipped it. From it he pulled out a handful of shiny green shirts. Khalid squinted at the logo on one, which was framed with Arabic script. 'It says *Shabab ul-Nasr*!'

'What does that mean?' asked Junayd.

'It means The Victory Boys!' exclaimed Khalid.

'Wicked!' said Ibrahim approvingly. 'Where did you get those?'

'Just found a good place,' smiled Saleem. 'The Imam gave us the money, you should thank him.'

'Just your *du'as*, please,' said a quiet voice from behind them.

'Imam!' called the boys in unison.

'*As-salamu 'alaykum*,' he said, opening his jacket to reveal a garish lime green shirt. 'I've come to give my support. But I can't fit into one of *those* green shirts; I'll wear this one instead.'

A few of the boys smiled uncertainly, wondering if this was some sort of joke. The rest of them just stared.

'Why are you looking at me like that – you are surprised to see me? You know how much I love a game of football!' added the Imam playfully.

After an impatient wait outside the Hilsham gates, they were finally swung open at 9.30 and the boys burst through. Underfoot the ground felt firm, with the grass short and perfect for quick passing.

'Khalid, you organise a warm-up,' instructed Saleem. 'I'm just going to get us registered.'

Imam Munieb accompanied him to a table fronted with a sign: REGISTER HERE. Behind it were two grumpy looking men sifting haphazardly through clipboards full of paper.

'Name,' said the older of the two.

'Er, Saleem Miah.'

'Is that *your* name?' sniggered the younger man, looking up.

'Not *your* name you dope,' the older one mocked. 'Your team name!'

'Oh,' replied Saleem, caught off guard. 'Er, *Shabab ul-Nasr.*'

'What?!' exclaimed the older man. 'Is that another of your names? Are you trying to wind us up?'

'Don't be a ...' began Saleem angrily, catching himself just in time.

'Don't be a *what*?'

Saleem took a deep breath.

'Would you like me to point out our team name on your paper, Sir?' he offered, in the calmest and politest voice he could muster.

The older man eyeballed him.

'Knock yourself out,' he growled, thrusting a clipboard at him with a list of team names attached.

'You're most kind,' replied Saleem, beginning to feel in control of the situation. He pointed to two names on the sheet.

'Here's our 'A' team, here's our ...'

'Read and sign these forms,' interrupted the man. 'Here's a fixture list. *Good luck,*' he added through gritted teeth.

'Have a nice day!' smiled Saleem sarcastically.

'*Ahsanta,*' approved Imam Munieb. 'You did very well there. I do not know about these people, what their problem is.'

'Who knows,' said Saleem. 'I was pretty close to losing it there for a second. Actually I'm really surprised I didn't!'

'*Mashallah,*' replied the Imam. 'It takes a real man to control his anger, and most men cannot. Unbelievable rewards in Islam for this self-control, I tell you.'

Saleem smiled. He felt a genuine peace inside him. He stopped to look around and take in his surroundings. The sun was already high in the clear blue sky, and the breeze today was calming in itself. When he was ready, he called the boys to finish their warm-up and make a semi-circle around him.

'OK boys, here's where we're at. 'A' team, you're in Group Three. 'B' team, you're in Group Two. Four teams in each group, so three matches each, then the semis, then the final. If I've understood this correctly you can only play each other if you meet in the final, so *inshallah* that'll be a happy ending and there'll only be us and the trophy still hanging around by then! Everyone feeling confident? Good ...'

Did I just say inshallah? thought Saleem.

Abdullah was studying, as usual.

From over his shoulder, Junayd saw that he had a list of the groups. He had highlighted all of the matches involving the 'B' team, for whom he had been selected as a sub.

'You're in the same group as Sedgecombe Shuttles!' announced Junayd.

'Yes,' nodded Abdullah. 'We're playing them first.'

'Well, watch out. They're good! My friend Jake plays for them. He scored forty-eight goals last season. They won the league.'

'I see,' replied Abdullah seriously, as if processing this information as a set of important and useable facts. In truth, he was trying not to sound worried.

'Well,' said Junayd, attempting to put a rather more positive spin on things, 'at least once you've played them, you'll know how high the standard is. I reckon the other games will be much easier.'

The 'B' team's game against Sedgecombe was the first fixture on Pitch Two. As they prepared to kick off, the 'A' team's support was nowhere to be seen.

They were far too interested in checking out two of their upcoming opponents, AFC Hilsham and Old Roar Rovers, who were battling it out on Pitch Three.

'This lot aren't very good,' declared Khalid confidently.

No one said anything, but they were inclined to agree with him.

'Excuse me, *ya Shabab*!' came a voice from behind them. 'How about supporting your brothers? We are on Pitch Two.'

Imam Munieb's expression indicated that he was not really offering them a choice, and they took a last lingering look at the action from their group before trotting over to watch the 'B' team.

The 'B' team were in some trouble when they arrived. Junayd's friend Jake had just slammed a shot into the top corner of the goal, to huge cheers from a sizeable Sedgecombe support. The score had reached 3-0 after only five minutes.

'Half-time,' announced the referee, after three short blasts on his whistle.

'OK boys,' said Saleem calmly as the boys sank to the floor around him. 'Remember this was always going to be challenging. Keep trying your hardest and don't lose heart. You'll see when you watch this lot against the other teams that you've actually done quite well. They're a good side, trust me. Test yourself in the second half and see if you can keep them out. Get into the tackles, don't give them any space, and you'll see them start to get frustrated. Right, come on, it's a quick change around – put your drinks down and off you go.'

'*Bismillah*,' added Imam Munieb, as the 'B' team returned to the pitch.

As the 'A' team boys limbered up ready for their game, there was a tiny cheer from Pitch Three. Old Roar Rovers had scored. A few moments later the final whistle blew to put them at the top of the group with a 1-0 win.

'Who are we playing again?' asked Ali, who kept checking his shoelaces and biting his nails.

'Milton Blaze,' said Junayd.

'What a silly name,' sniggered Ibrahim.

'They probably think *our* name is silly,' replied Junayd.

'We do,' said a shaven-headed boy in a red and white striped shirt and an unusually large captain's armband. 'What the hell does it mean anyway?'

'It means Victory Boys,' asserted Khalid. 'You'll be finding out why in the next ten minutes. Hey, you need me to cut a couple of metres off that armband of yours? It's just I'd hate to see you fall over under the weight of it.'

The boy glared at him.

'We'll see who's laughing at the end.'

'I'm laughing *now*!' teased Khalid. 'That armband! Hey, you're not going swimming are you? You'll need another one, you know.'

The Milton Blaze captain glowered and spun around.

'Come on boys!' he roared. 'Let's teach this lot a lesson!'

That exchange set the scene for a very competitive opening to the match. Tackles flew in from both sets of players (especially from Junayd, who did not hesitate whenever the ball was there to be won) and the referee had to whistle for several free kicks in the first few minutes.

'Keep your cool, boys,' urged Saleem, who had jogged over as soon as the 'B' team game had finished. 'It's the football that's gonna hurt 'em, not you!'

Ali had begun to shake off his nerves and was now proving a nuisance to the Blaze team by taking up a wide position whenever they had the ball.

'Pick him up,' instructed their captain (who, like Khalid, was also a defender).

'He's a forward,' returned their midfielder, all flame-hair and freckles. 'Why should *I* mark him?'

With such uncertainty – and a total lack of marking – it wasn't long before Ali got a clear run at goal. He drew in the Blaze captain and – just as his opponent attempted a tackle – slid the ball to an unmarked Ibrahim, who drove it into the net past their shell-shocked keeper.

'*Yes!*' cried the boys, all sprinting over to congratulate Ibrahim.

'*EA-SY! EA-SY!*' chanted Khalid.

'Hey!' called Saleem. 'There's a long way to go yet! Concentrate!'

Saleem was right. Milton Blaze were far from defeated and launched a wave of attacks. Khalid and Yunus worked valiantly to repel them but twice their slightly built (and electrifyingly quick) forward burst free into space. First, he was denied by a quick interception from Hasan, and then by a fine save, Hasan diving to his left to turn the ball around the post.

'Great save Hasan!' called the watching 'B' team, who had shrugged off their defeat (4–0 in the end) to support their friends.

The pressure persisted, and even Ali was doggedly working to defend his goal.

With only a couple of minutes remaining, Khalid intercepted a stray pass and pushed the ball into space ahead of him. He skipped past an opponent and looked up. Suddenly the whole pitch had opened up for him. Only the rival captain stood between Khalid and a shot at goal.

As the Blaze boy charged toward Khalid, he spotted the Milton Blaze goalkeeper some distance from his goal line. Just as the opposing team's captain was set to launch himself into the tackle, Khalid leaned back and hit the ball high, sailing over the head of his rival, over the despairing jump of the goalkeeper, and into the net.

'*WHAT A GOAL*!!' Khalid congratulated himself, as his whole team and support roared as well.

'Who did you say would be laughing?' he called out in the direction of the Blaze captain, cupping his hand around his ear as he had seen the professional players do on the T.V.

His opponent's face wore a furious look.

'Leave it, Khalid!' commanded Saleem. 'We gotta keep it tight now, let's keep what we've got. Everyone hold your positions, yeah?'

Milton Blaze had not given up, and renewed their pressure on Hasan's goal. Yet once again, Khalid broke clear and raced away with the ball. But this time the collective hunger for a decisive third goal carried all of the boys forward with him.

'Pass, pass it!' called Yunus, who had overlapped Khalid on his left.

'Give it wide!' screamed Ali, on the right wing.

Khalid noticed Ibrahim and Junayd in support on either side of him too. There were suddenly too many options to consider. Before he had decided what to do, the ball had been nicked off Khalid's toe by the Blaze captain.

Suddenly, it was *his* turn for a free run on goal. The *Shabab* boys desperately scampered back but they could only watch in horror as the Blaze captain rounded Hasan and drove the ball into the net. 2–1.

'COME *ON*!' came the war cry from the Blaze team, and now it was Team *Shabab*'s turn to be shell-shocked. From feeling they had won the game, they now began to panic that they were about to throw it away.

None of this helped them to follow or even *remember* Saleem's instructions. Ibrahim was back desperately defending instead of holding his position in attack, and Ali was so close to his own goal that Hasan could barely see the action.

With so many bodies in the goalmouth, there was inevitable confusion when Milton Blaze launched one last attack, swinging a high ball towards Hasan's goal. It should have been a simple catch for Hasan but his path was obstructed by Ali, Khalid, Yunus *and* Ibrahim, all of whom jumped for the ball at the same time. The entire team collided with one another. As they did so, the nippy Blaze forward drove home the loose ball for the equaliser.

2–2.

The final whistle blew.

'*No!*' cried everyone.

'What happened?' said Hasan, shaking his head in bewilderment.

'I'm sorry,' said a smug voice, 'I must be going deaf. Didn't you say you would be laughing now? It's just ... I can't hear anything.'

'You got lucky,' Khalid scowled at the Blaze captain. 'But I meant I'll be laughing at the end of the group when we go to the semis and you go home.'

'Khalid, shut it man!' said Saleem. 'You need to spend less time using your mouth and more time using your brain.'

The Blaze captain chuckled and trotted off happily to celebrate his team's unlikely draw with his mates.

Saleem saw that Khalid looked a little hurt and he remembered Imam Munieb's advice about criticism.

'We *all* need to use our brains, Khalid,' he added. 'Especially me. I should have put on a sub who I could have told to stay in position. That's what went wrong out there at the end. If you're all defending, who are we going to pass the ball up to, to break free from the pressure?'

'If I can say something,' said Imam Munieb to the boys as he gestured towards Saleem. 'This man is your leader. He gives you instructions; you trust that they are the right ones. What I have seen here is very much like the Battle of Uhud. On that day the Muslims were winning when some of them decided they knew better than the Prophet Muhammad, *sallallahu alayhi wa sallam*. They ignored their instructions, left their positions and tried to score the greater victory ... they ended up losing.'

'But *we* didn't lose,' said Khalid.

'Do you feel as if you *won?*' countered the Imam.

'Two minutes gents,' came a voice. It was the Pitch Two referee. 'You're on again next.'

'What?' protested Ibrahim. 'Give me a chance to catch my breath! Don't we get a break?'

'You wanna start as sub?' asked Saleem.

'Er, no, I'll be fine,' Ibrahim quickly reassured him.

'OK then. So listen boys,' Saleem continued, 'hold your positions this time. Trust your teammates to do their jobs. It's good to work hard for one another, but remember how we do that?'

'By making space,' said Junayd.

'Got it, little bruv,' replied Saleem with a smile. 'On a football pitch that's the best support you can give.'

10. Coach Saleem's Masterstroke

Before the 'A' team had chance to fully recover, they were back in action, this time against Old Roar Rovers.

Buoyed by their earlier victory, and expecting to find the *Shabab* boys in some disarray after their capitulation in the previous match, the group leaders took the game to their opponents from the off. Hasan had to spectacularly deny them an early lead with an acrobatic fingertip save over the bar.

Despite a slow start Team *Shabab* were looking far better organised. Khalid now led by example. He called instructions to his team mates, and encouraged them to support one another. He was quick to remind them of where they should and shouldn't be too.

At half-time the game was goalless, but both teams had enjoyed good possession. Keeping the ball was not going to be enough to progress though, and Saleem knew it.

'We've got to win this game,' he told Imam Munieb.

'A draw is no good?'

'I don't think so. If that Blaze team win their next two games we won't be able to catch them.'

'How are we getting on then?' asked a friendly voice. It was Mr Bateman, his smile beaming at them under a pair of dark sunglasses. He had a green scarf draped loosely around his neck.

'Hello,' replied the Imam cheerfully, 'I'm so glad you could make it!'

'Oh, I like a game of football, me. You were doing *me* a favour, telling me about this tournament. Besides,' he added in a mischievous voice, 'it got me out of a trip to the supermarket. *Now then*, what's the score?'

'It is nought, nought,' said Imam Munieb.

'Nil-nil, eh?' said Mr Bateman. 'Who's going to grab that winning goal then eh? Got any good subs?'

'I think we've got the players on the pitch to do it,' said Saleem.

'Never underestimate a speedy substitute when the other team are tired,' advised Mr Bateman.

'It's our team who are tired,' observed Saleem. 'We're playing two games back to back. This other lot have just had a rest!'

'I'm ready to go on,' said Faris, who had been listening hopefully to their conversation. 'I'm fast, too!'

Saleem looked down at Faris, who was hopping up and down eagerly on his little legs.

'We'll leave it for a couple of minutes bruv,' he said, though with less certainty than before.

Team *Shabab* were continuing to knock the ball about neatly and, whenever they did lose it, Junayd was tigerish in winning it back again.

Time had ebbed away. But just as the game appeared set to finish goalless, an Old Roar defender lunged in on Ali and conceded a free kick, a few feet from the touchline.

Saleem looked again at Faris. An idea had occurred to him.

'*Ref! Sub!*' he called.

The referee looked at his watch.

'You'll have to be quick,' he warned.

'*Timewasting, ref!*' called the Old Roar manager.

'They're just playing for the draw now,' complained one of their supporters.

'Junayd,' beckoned Saleem. 'Well played bruv, off you come now.'

There were a few bemused noises among the *Shabab* team as their industrious midfielder trotted off the pitch, surprised to be the player replaced.

Saleem whispered a few quick instructions in Faris' ear, and the smallest player in the 'A' team sprinted on to the pitch. He delivered an impossibly quick message to Ali, and then took up a position on the far side of Ibrahim. Faris stood so close that Ibrahim complained.

'Hey! Not so close, Faris! What are you doing, *marking* me?'

'When Ali hits the cross,' Faris mumbled, 'run to the near post.'

Saleem had called Yunus and Khalid to him, and now they ran forward too, taking up a central position just a little further back than Ibrahim. The entire *Shabab* team were in the opposition half.

It was now or never.

'Mark 'em up boys,' growled the Old Roar manager. 'There's some big lads in there. Don't let 'em win the aerial ball ... '

The referee blew his whistle amid much jostling between the tall *Shabab* boys and their markers. Just at the moment

Ali made contact with the dead ball, Ibrahim, Khalid and Yunus darted to the near post. Every one of the Old Roar defenders followed in hot pursuit.

Ali's crossed ball cleared all of them. The ball dropped neatly onto the head of Faris at the back post, who nodded it into the net with the simplest of headers.

'*YES!*' came the ecstatic cry from the *Shabab* boys. They raced to leap on Faris, just as his team mates had done back in that first ever session in the mosque yard.

'Oh-ho, that is *genius!*' purred Mr Bateman.

'*Mashallah!*' agreed Imam Munieb.

'Did you *tell* them to do that?' Junayd asked his brother.

Saleem just smiled.

'*Alhamdulillah*. That was beautiful, wasn't it!'

Old Roar Rovers barely had time to kick off again before the referee blew the final whistle. The sound signalled the first *Shabab* victory of the tournament, which was greeted with great cheers.

'Well done, boys!' congratulated Mr Bateman. He turned to Ali. 'That was a fan*tastic* cross, young man!'

'Thanks,' replied Ali, remembering now where he had seen this man before. 'Did you come to watch *us?*'

Mr Bateman nodded cheerfully.

'But we smashed your greenhouse,' added Ali.

'Yes I remember that,' replied Mr Bateman. 'But I can't see any greenhouses here so I should think you're quite safe this time.'

The boys ambled over to Pitch Two, where the 'B' team were in action. On this occasion the teams were evenly matched, and the score was drifting towards a 0-0 draw.

'Do your substitution trick again!' Junayd encouraged Saleem.

'I don't know if that'll work here bruv,' replied Saleem, wondering who in the 'B' team might be able to deliver a ball as accurately as Ali had. 'But I do need to make sure everyone in the squad gets a game. Where's the other sub anyway?'

'Abdullah!' yelled Khalid. 'What are you doing over on Pitch Three? Come here!' he beckoned.

Abdullah trotted over.

'What is it?' he said, with a hint of annoyance. 'I was just keeping an eye on your group. You *do* realise that if you and Milton Blaze win your remaining games, you're going to have to beat them on goal difference, *don't* you? And *they* are winning 4–0 right now!'

Abdullah, who was no longer in the slightest bit interested in actually playing football, proceeded to explain. After their current match Milton Blaze would face Old Roar Rovers. A win for Old Roar, or a draw, would mean *Shabab* 'A' would qualify for the semi-finals with a win in their last game. But if Milton Blaze won, the *Shabab* team would have to win by at least as many goals as the Blaze team could muster in their two games. Which was already *four*.

Old Roar Rovers were no match for Milton Blaze who emerged easy victors, 2–0.

'That means,' said Abdullah to the *Shabab* players as they limbered up, 'that you must beat AFC Hilsham by six goals.'

The boys looked at one another nervously.

'And,' he reminded them helpfully, 'you've only got ten minutes.'

The rest of the 'B' team had wandered over to lend their support. They had ended their own campaign with a second 0–0 draw to finish third in their group. The group had been won at a canter by the Sedgecombe Shuttles. They remained respectfully silent as Saleem delivered the most important pre-match team talk of his coaching tenure to date.

'OK boys,' he said encouragingly, 'this is it. We gotta do this the hard way, right?'

The boys nodded.

'We can do this,' asserted Khalid. 'Come on boys, we've seen this lot. They're rubbish. Let's nail 'em from the start.'

'Yunus, I want you to stay back at all times,' instructed Saleem, 'but Khalid – we need to get a shed-full of goals here. Try and get up and down as much as you can. Ali, they're a small team. Get some high balls into Ibrahim. Junayd, some tough tackles from you and they won't even want the ball again. Get stuck in. Hard but fair boys, you get me? Ten minutes of giving it everything you've got, yeah?'

'*Come on!*' cried Khalid, a fiercely determined look on his face.

The Hilsham team did not know what had hit them. Within the first ten seconds of the game, a bulldozing tackle from Junayd won the ball from his opposite number. And, just as Saleem had said they would, the rest of the team shrank away from the action.

Ibrahim headed two goals in quick succession; soon after Ali waltzed through a series of half-hearted tackles to make it 3–0. At that point the watching Milton Blaze team started to look worried.

Khalid added the fourth just before half-time. He tapped into an empty net after Ali had tricked his way towards goal and poked the ball through the keeper's legs.

The Hilsham players, already out of the tournament, were even less interested in the second half. Ibrahim added two goals (one with either foot) and set up Junayd for a seventh just before the final whistle.

The *Shabab* boys left the field weary but delighted.

'That was classy,' said Ibrahim, patting each of his team-mates on the back.

Khalid noticed the Milton Blaze captain heading towards him.

Here we go again, he thought. He barely had the energy left to say anything to his rival, despite having emerged victorious in the end.

However, to his surprise, as the Blaze captain got to within a few metres, he extended his hand to Khalid.

'You guys were awesome out there just now,' he said. 'You've got a good chance in this tournament. Win it for us, yeah?'

Khalid was quite taken aback as he shook the boy's hand.

'Er, yeah, hope so ...' he said, 'your team made it tough for us though. Maybe next year, yeah?'

'Hope so,' nodded the captain, shaking hands with each member of the *Shabab* squad before jogging back to his own team.

'Now *that* was classy,' announced Mr Bateman.

11. A Tale of Two Penalties

Saleem and Abdullah were on a scouting mission on Pitch Four. They were going to watch the final group game.

'I've just been over to the results table,' said Abdullah. 'This is an unusual group. If this score stays the same, all of the teams will have won one, drawn one and lost one. Four points apiece.'

'So who wins the group?' asked Saleem.

'I'm just adding up the goals now,' replied Abdullah, his tongue protruding from his lips as he totalled the numbers up in his head.

'I make it *this* team ... Tophill United,' he announced, pointing to their name on his fixture list.

'Are they one of the teams playing now?'

'Yes, they're the team in blue. It's 1–1 at the moment, but if the other team score, we'll be playing them instead.' He looked Saleem in the eye. 'It's exciting, isn't it?'

'Whatever you say bro,' replied Saleem, raising an eyebrow. 'I prefer to look at what's going on *on* the pitch. See who their best players are.'

'I can ask their manager who's been playing well, if you like? You know, who has scored the most goals, made the most tackles etcetera?'

'Um ... no.'

'OK boys,' announced Saleem with a clap of the hands, 'We're playing Tophill United in the semis. Abdullah can tell you their history in a moment if you like, but I'm gonna tell you that they're there for the taking. Got a lad in the midfield who's quite tricky – Junayd, he's yours. Stick tight, don't give him room to breathe. You boys play like you did in the last game and a place in the final is yours, *inshallah*.'

Imam Munieb nodded approvingly. Saleem cut an impressive figure as team coach.

It was a shame, he thought, that his parents were not here to see him now.

This gave him an idea.

'Straight in boys!' cried Khalid, clapping his hands together ferociously.

Ibrahim and Ali kicked off and knocked the ball back to Junayd. Immediately he pushed it wide, where Ali had reappeared. Ali whipped in a menacing cross in the direction of Ibrahim's head.

Ibrahim had stolen a yard on the Tophill defender, who suddenly realised that the ball was arrowing straight to the striker's head. In desperation, he reached out for Ibrahim's shirt and yanked him back. The pull unbalanced Ibrahim and he fell to the ground. A whistle blew.

'*Penalty*!' called the referee.

'*No way*!' protested the Tophill players. 'Olly never touched him!'

Ibrahim shrugged his shoulders.

'You know it was a foul,' he told the defender, who scowled at him, then at the referee.

'Who takes?' asked Khalid in the direction of Saleem.

'You,' answered the coach. 'Decide what you're going to do with it and don't change your mind.'

I'm going to blast it down the middle, thought Khalid.

He placed the ball on the spot and waited. The referee blew the whistle.

Khalid ran up and gave the ball an almighty thump.

The goalkeeper, who had decided to wait until Khalid kicked the ball, remained rooted to the spot. The ball hit him like a rocket – straight in the face. He fell backwards into the goal as the ball rebounded down and trickled along the goal line.

The boys stood motionless as gasps and shrieks came from the Tophill support. Their defender, Olly, eager to stop the play and protect his goalkeeper, picked up the ball.

The referee's whistle sounded again.

'Stop, move out of the way!' he called, rushing over to inspect the condition of the goalkeeper, who was lying prone in the net.

An anxious woman – presumably the goalkeeper's mother – ran over to the goalmouth and bent over the boy.

'Josh! Joshy?' she cried. 'Are you all right? Speak to me, Joshy!'

They heard a groan from the boy, and immediately there was a palpable sense of relief that Josh was, at least, still alive.

'You're bleeding, Joshy!' squealed the woman. 'Oh gosh! We must get you to hospital!'

'I think we should phone an ambulance,' said Imam Munieb, who had hurried over to check that the boy was OK. 'Would you like me to do this?'

'Oh, yes I think so,' said Josh's mother, pulling frantically at her hair. 'Please, if you would do that, thank you ...'

Time had frozen for the *Shabab* team, all of whom were in shock at the state of the goalkeeper. Khalid, especially, was shaken by what had happened.

'Is he going to be OK?' he whispered to the referee. 'I didn't mean to hurt him, you know.'

'Just an accident son,' replied the referee. 'I think he'll be OK.'

'Er, ref ...' began Olly, cautiously. 'What happens now?'

'We're trying to call an ambulance,' replied the referee.

'No, no, I didn't mean that,' the defender continued. 'I meant, when the game starts again. I picked up the ball, didn't I? Is it another penalty?'

'Oh, goodness me, I hadn't thought of that,' said the ref. 'Well, I suppose I hadn't stopped the play, so ... I don't have much of a choice ...'

'That's not fair,' complained another of the Tophill players. 'He was only trying to protect Josh!'

Khalid thought for a moment and he remembered the Milton Blaze captain.

It's time to do something *classy*, he thought.

'We won't score,' he said. 'I'll just kick it wide.'

And that is precisely what happened. Once the ambulance had arrived and ferried the Tophill goalkeeper to hospital, Khalid deliberately missed the spot kick. The crowd applauded him, and the game continued.

Team *Shabab* had trouble matching the pace of their frenetic start.

Junayd worked tirelessly to ensure that the Tophill playmaker was not given time on the ball to do any damage. But Khalid was not his usual imposing self, and without his drive the team coasted to half-time without a goal.

The second half began with Junayd in typically bustling fashion, harrying Tophill's star player. He had been marshalling his opponent superbly when he stumbled over a divot and pulled up clutching his hamstring.

'*Owww*!' he grunted.

'You alright, bruv?' called Saleem. 'Run it off, yeah?'

Junayd flexed his leg muscles and winced.

'Ow, I don't think I can,' he replied.

'OK bro, off you come,' instructed his brother briskly. 'Ismail, up you get! You're on!'

Ismail was the largest squad member by some way, and his facial hair meant he was often mistaken for an older boy. He cut an intimidating figure on the pitch, but he wasn't the quickest.

It only took a minute for the Tophill midfielder to recognise that he was going to have a bit more freedom with the ball.

The ball broke to him in midfield and he flicked the ball past Ismail's right side and then outpaced him on his left. Once inside the penalty area, he dummied to shoot, inviting a desperate sliding challenge from Khalid. The Tophill midfielder took a second touch and Khalid's leg careered into his, sending him tumbling to the turf. Khalid held up his hands, knowing exactly what was to come next.

The whistle sounded again.

'*Penalty*!' called the referee.

There were no protests from the *Shabab* team. All the noise came from the excited Tophill players, who now threatened to take the lead with only two minutes remaining.

The Tophill midfielder dusted himself down and placed the ball on the spot.

'*Come on Hasan,*' urged Khalid, willing his friend to undo his own mistake.

'*Come on lad!*' called Mr Bateman.

'*Say Bismillah!*' said Imam Munieb.

The whistle blew.

'*Bismillah,*' breathed Hasan.

The Tophill midfielder advanced toward the ball, then checked his run with the intention of fooling Hasan. When he finally made contact with the ball, it arrowed towards the corner of the goal.

Hasan leapt to his left and, with the very tips of his fingers, deflected the ball around the post.

'*What a save*!' cooed the players and spectators in unison. The penalty taker shook his head in disbelief. A few of his team mates even applauded.

'*Mashallah*!' cried Saleem and the Imam together.

'That boy's the new Gordon Banks, I'm telling you,' said Mr Bateman.

'Gordon *who*?' said Junayd.

12. Last Legs

What a reprieve!

Buoyed by Hasan's wonder save, the *Shabab* boys played with a renewed confidence. They sensed that they were destined to win the match.

'*Shoot!*' called Mr Bateman, whenever Ibrahim or Ali had a sight of goal. 'That boy between the sticks *isn't* a goalie, remember?'

Both boys took the advice and tried several shots from around the edge of the penalty area. But their efforts sailed wide of the post, over the crossbar, or tamely into the grateful hands of Tophill's makeshift goalie.

Saleem was thinking hard. The only idea he had right now was to send on a fresh pair of legs.

'Faris,' he said. 'You're going on soon, get warmed up.'

But Faris' introduction was to come even earlier than planned.

Ibrahim had over-stretched for the ball and was now sitting upright on the grass, gingerly rubbing the underside of his leg.

'I've pulled a muscle,' he moaned. 'I don't think I can play on.'

Saleem sighed. He wondered if he would have enough fit players to get through the inevitable extra time period, let alone play in the final should they get there.

'OK Faris,' he said. 'Straight up front, run around and make a nuisance of yourself.'

'*Shoot on sight!*' Mr Bateman implored him.

However, there were no more chances in normal time. The six remaining boys gathered around Saleem for a quick pep-talk before the start of extra time.

'OK boys,' said their coach, 'I've been told you've only got two minutes each way. That's ... well, that's no time at all. You guys look *exhausted* and I think our best bet is penalties now. We've got Hasan, the best goalie in the tournament *mashallah*; they don't even have their proper goalie.

'Keep it tight and, if in doubt, put a ball into space for Faris to run on to – he's the only one who's still fresh. Everyone OK?

'Come on then boys, get out there, four more minutes, yeah?'

As the extra time period unfolded, it was clear that both teams were suffering from tiredness, and even Tophill's star midfielder was struggling to maintain his high standards. Twice Ismail outwitted him and came away with the ball.

As instructed, the *Shabab* boys played safely, until Yunus found himself in a tight corner with no one to pass to. He launched the ball up the field in the direction of Faris.

Faris took the ball down expertly and pushed it past his nearest opponent who, sensing that Faris was easily quick enough to leave him for dead, stuck out a tired leg and tripped him up. Once more, the whistle blew.

'Free kick!' called the referee.

'How long's left, ref?' asked Khalid.

'About thirty seconds,' came the reply. 'Then penalties, if it's still level.'

'Should we do, er, what we did last time?' Ali asked Khalid, trying to avoid being overheard by the opposition.

'I've got an idea,' said Khalid. He bounded over to Ali and whispered in his ear.

'Yunus, Ismail, get up there!' he ordered. 'Faris, you stay back, just in case they break.'

'But I'm not a defender!' protested Faris, who was secretly hoping he might get his second goal of the tournament.

'But *I'm* the captain,' asserted Khalid.

Faris accepted this point and jogged back to his own half. He stood nervously, praying that he would not be called upon to repel a counter-attack.

Saleem, who had no idea what Khalid was up to, folded his arms and looked on, intrigued.

Ali stood over the ball just a few yards inside the Tophill half, on the far left-hand side. Khalid, Yunus and Ismail had arranged themselves some way to the right of the Tophill goal. They began to jostle their opponents.

'Let's win this header boys,' called Khalid. 'Last chance! Get your head on it, whatever happens!'

Sensing the importance of the moment, the Tophill defenders got as tight as they could to the *Shabab* boys, determined to keep out the aerial attack.

When the referee's whistle blew, the three *Shabab* players suddenly stopped their jostling and turned to watch as Ali, with a huge run-up, leathered the ball goalwards.

'Watch the shot!' called a voice from somewhere among the Tophill crowd, but by then it was too late.

The ball flew into the left side of the net; the goalkeeper was rooted to the spot like everyone else.

A terrific roar from Team *Shabab*'s exhausted players and modest army of supporters ensued. Mr Bateman was now jumping up and down in a manner that belied his senior years.

'*I've never seen anything like it!*' he cried. 'That boy's got a *wand* for a foot, I'm telling you!'

Imam Munieb had no idea what Mr Bateman was talking about, but he slapped him happily on the back anyway.

'*Mashallah!*' he said approvingly.

Imam Munieb was somewhat relieved, too. It would have been awfully inconvenient if the guests he had recently invited had arrived to find the team eliminated from the tournament.

Aha, he thought, as his guests came into view, approaching the jubilant scenes on Pitch Two. *Here they are.*

It was Saleem's mother and father.

13. Genius

'*As-salamu 'alaykum!*' smiled Imam Munieb. 'I'm so pleased you could come.'

'*Wa'alaykum as-salam,*' replied Mr Miah with a wide smile as he shook the Imam's hand. 'This is a big surprise. You say my son is playing in a football match? I didn't know ...'

'*Ubba!*' called Junayd, staggering over as quickly as he could. 'I didn't know you knew about this.'

'Well of course I didn't know,' said his father, feeling embarrassed in front of the Imam. 'You didn't tell me, *did* you?'

'I thought you would be too busy,' replied Junayd.

'*Kita khorsot?*' gasped Mrs Miah, noticing her son's limp.

'I pulled a muscle. It's OK *Umma*, but I don't think I can play any more today.'

'Oh dear, that's a shame,' said Mr Miah, more to the Imam than his son. 'We came 'specially to see you!'

'Well,' said the Imam, pointing behind him, 'you can still watch your son in action. Your *other* son. He's over there, talking to his team.'

Mr Miah looked beyond the Imam and, to his utter surprise, saw his eldest son looking animated and speaking earnestly to half a dozen boys in their green football strip.

'*Saleem?*' he said. 'What is he doing here?'

'He is the coach of the team!'

'He's a *genius*,' added Mr Bateman, joining the conversation. 'Some of the calls he's made today have been nothing short of perfection. And of course the boys have played wonderfully, but that's largely down to your boy as well, if you ask me. And I'm told he even got the kit for them too. What an organiser, eh? You must be very proud.'

Saleem's father stood, staring, shaking his head slightly as he tried to make sense of what he was seeing, and of what he had just been told.

Saleem, a *genius*?

'We're down to the last game boys, and whatever happens in this final, you've done brilliantly,' Saleem said to the *Shabab* boys. 'I mean it. I've wanted to be out there kicking and heading every ball myself, but you guys have done it better than I could've anyway. And your decision making has been top-notch! Khalid man, great idea for that free-kick. You won it for us there bro. That's what I was talking about – more thinking. You've gotta be confident now, doesn't matter that we're down two players, we've got enough to win this final.'

'Who are we playing, then?' Ali asked Saleem.

'Sedgecombe Shuttles,' answered Abdullah before the coach could speak. 'A perfect record: four matches, four wins, twelve goals scored, none conceded. They'll be the favourites, on paper.'

'Do you actually *want* us to win?' Khalid confronted him.

'Er, of course,' replied Abdullah. 'But one has to admire a perfect record.'

'Hey, Junayd!' said a voice. 'You guys made the final? Wow!'

An athletically built boy with blond hair was jogging over. It was Jake, his friend from school.

'Yeah we did, although *I* didn't ... I'm injured.'

'Oh no, that's a shame. Is that your team over there then?'

'Yeah, and that's my brother,' Junayd pointed out proudly. 'He's the coach.'

'Do you play for that Shuttles team then?' asked Ibrahim, who had become bored of sitting on the grass and had limped over to join them.

'Yeah, that's right,' replied Jake, uncertain as to who was addressing him.

'Oh sorry,' said Junayd, 'This is Ibrahim. Remember I told you about ...'

'Oh yeah, Ibrahim,' nodded Jake. 'Junayd told me about you. So what school do you go to?'

'I don't,' replied Ibrahim. 'I mean I don't go to school; I'm home schooled.'

'Oh,' said Jake, not sure what to say next on that subject, 'but you're a good footballer, right? That guy over there,' he said, pointing at Abdullah, 'told me we're the joint top scorers in the tournament!'

'Really?' said Ibrahim, impressed. 'He might've told me that! Oh well, I can't challenge you for that honour now I'm afraid; looks like I'll be sitting out the final.'

'You're both injured?'

'Yeah, pulled a muscle.' Ibrahim thought for a moment. 'How's that then, Junayd. We entered the team in this tournament and now we get to sit on the sidelines and watch the final.'

Imam Munieb and Saleem's parents had wandered over to where their son was just finishing his pre-match team talk. They stood a little way back, out of sight.

' ... let's keep to our positions, and give it everything we got! Come on then boys! *Bismillah!*'

Saleem's father was finding it hard to reconcile the young man speaking such passionate and inspirational words right in front of his eyes, with the lazy, troublesome son he thought he knew and found quite hard to like.

As the boys jogged over to the pitch for a light warm-up, Saleem glanced behind him. Now it was his turn to be surprised.

His mother smiled at him, dabbing at a tear with the corner of her *shaaree*.

'Hello Saleem,' said his father in a quiet tone. 'They tell me you're a genius?'

14. David and Goliath

A man with a huge red umbrella approached the modest *Shabab* support.

'You don't mind if I stand here, do you?' he asked them. 'Only there's so many of us, you see, we can't all fit together over there.'

He pointed to the vast congregation of Sedgecombe supporters, most of whom were clad in the red of their team's colours. It was really quite a sight.

'Please, you are very welcome,' gestured Imam Munieb with an outstretched hand.

'You expecting rain later?' asked Mr Bateman impishly.

Before the umbrella man could respond, a chant issued forth from the red army assembled on the opposite side of the pitch.

'*SEDGE-COMBE*!!' they cried, accompanied by loud rhythmic clapping and two men pounding large tin drums secured around their necks. '*SEDGE-COMBE*!!'

'Is this a professional team?' joked Mr Bateman, although he almost began to wonder if he might be right.

Saleem was a little discomfited by all of the noise, which he had not been aware of in any of the Shuttles' previous matches. He noticed that the boys were looking to him for reassurance. He shrugged dismissively as if to tell them that the noise was of no importance.

When play got underway, it soon became clear how Sedgecombe Shuttles had accomplished their 'perfect record'. Their passing was slick, their movement off the ball extremely sharp, and they were abnormally big boys.

The largest of them was named Will. He was playing as a solitary defender, and he towered over Faris.

'It's like David and *Goliath*!' exclaimed Mr Bateman, rubbing his eyes.

'Yes, but remember who won *that* little battle,' smiled Imam Munieb.

'He plays at the back on his own,' said the umbrella man. 'He's good enough by himself.'

'He's *big* enough by himself,' said Mr Bateman.

Playing one at the back freed up the rest of the Shuttles' outfield players to set about pressurising the *Shabab* goal!

At the heart of their play was a boy named Zachary: a well-built midfielder with his hair in braids. All of the Shuttles' attacks seemed to go through him. He sprayed the ball to either wing with ease, and occasionally darted through the middle himself; either by playing a one-two or by feinting his way through alone.

Within the first minute Hasan had to deny him, firmly palming the ball around the post at the expense of a corner. Zachary then swung the ball in and Will, totally unchallenged, headed it against the crossbar.

'*OOOH*!!' came the cry from the Sedgecombe support as the ball bounced up and out of play.

From the goal kick Hasan played a short pass to Khalid, who tried to work the ball neatly from the back. Immediately the *Shabab* boys found themselves under intense pressure and Ismail conceded possession. Zachary flicked the ball wide, where their fleet-footed winger tore inside Yunus and crashed a shot goal-bound.

It looked for all the world that it would slam into the net, yet a diving Hasan stretched and somehow diverted it around the post with the very tips of his fingers.

'*Brilliant save!*' called Mr Bateman. 'He's unbeatable, isn't he?'

There was generous applause all round – even from the Shuttles supporters.

'Phew, good save bro!' said Khalid gratefully, patting Hasan on the back as they prepared for the corner. '*Come on brothers*, get tight! Everyone mark a man and win your header!'

Zachary curled in a vicious in-swinging cross. It looked destined to meet the head of Will once more, until a gloved hand intervened and punched the ball clear.

'Well done *again*,' said Mr Bateman approvingly.

'We need to get into this game,' murmured Saleem nervously to himself. He looked around and saw Junayd and Ibrahim following the action with pained expressions. Behind them, on the sloping grass verge, sat his parents. Saleem was pleased that they had seen him in a positive light today, but he also felt that their presence was disrupting his thinking.

'I'm not sure what to do!' he confided to the Imam. 'Got no subs left, and these boys are *good*! Hasan's keeping them out so far, but ... there's a long way to go ... we're not even keeping the ball long enough to get *near* their goal!'

'*Mashallah*, whatever happens, they are learning important lessons today Coach Saleem,' replied Imam Munieb. 'I think you are too. Sometimes you need to be in a situation like this to work out what to do when things go against you. Sometimes you think the worst thing happened but actually it's the best thing for you, even if maybe it's hard to see that at the time. Anyway whatever happens is *qadrullah*. You can do your best to prepare – and you have done that, believe me, I have watched you. But you cannot change what is written.'

Saleem took a deep breath and accepted the words of the Imam.

There was no respite for the *Shabab* team on the pitch. Khalid struggled to keep pace with Jake and inadvertently tripped him just a few inches from the penalty area.

Faced with a free kick at such close range, Hasan set about organising a wall, but Khalid wasn't so keen.

'If we all get in this wall,' he argued, 'who's going to mark up all of their players?'

In the end Khalid and Ismail, the largest of the *Shabab* boys, formed a small blockade in front of Zachary.

Zachary looked set to pass the ball short to Jake. Yet when the whistle blew, he whipped a terrific shot around the two-man wall.

With astonishing reactions, Hasan flung himself to his left and tipped the ball behind for a corner.

There was a medley of admiring sounds and groans from all around the pitch. Zachary shook his head in disbelief.

Mr Bateman said nothing. This time even *he* had run out of superlatives. He simply joined in the head-shaking, patted the Imam on the back, and rubbed his hands with glee.

Some desperate tackles and blocks from Khalid and Yunus – and another solid stop from Hasan – helped Team

Shabab to limp to half-time, miraculously without having conceded a goal.

'Well done, boys,' Saleem encouraged them. 'Look at what you've done out there. Those boys have thrown *everything* at you and you're still standing, you're still fighting, you're still in with a chance. Sometimes it's just meant to be, you get me?

'Keep working hard because I tell you what: those boys are gonna start getting frustrated. You *know* it. They're gonna start to believe they can't score past you - and, *mashallah*, the way Hasan's playing, I don't think they ever will!'

'Can I say something?' asked Mr Bateman.

'Er, sure ...' said Saleem, a little surprised.

'I just want to say that you boys ... you've played this whole tournament in such a wonderful style. Even now, the way you're working together and digging in – you've got just as much class as these other boys, just in a different way. Now I tell you what,' he went on, 'I've been watching football longer than all of your ages put together. This team you're playing, they think it's all about whether they score. They haven't even given a thought about the possibility that *you* might score. You can catch them off guard, I'm telling you. Just keep believing in yourselves and you might spring a big surprise!'

Behind the team, Saleem's father listened to the words of this stranger. He wondered what it said about the community that he was the team's biggest fan. He only had to look at his two sons to see what this meant to them and what it was doing for their development as young men.

The boys, who had listened to all of Mr Bateman's speech, had by now almost forgotten the siege of the first half.

'We can do this!' affirmed Khalid. 'Come on brothers!'

'Come on!' cried his teammates and they jumped up determinedly to return to action.

As expected, the Shuttles immediately resumed their assault on the *Shabab* goal. But their efforts were beginning to fizzle out. First Hasan raced off his line to curtail a run from Zachary. Then the goalkeeper was out quickly again to save at the feet of Jake, as the striker dawdled when presented with a chance to shoot.

The Shuttles, for all of their flair on the pitch, were straining for new ideas. A momentary lapse from Will presented the ball to Faris on the halfway line. The tiny *Shabab* forward saw a chance to hammer it forwards and beat his giant marker for pace, but Will recovered in time to get the slightest of deflections and the ball trickled away for an unlikely *Shabab* corner.

In fact, it was the first time the *Shabab* team had even ventured into their opponents' half!

Suddenly, the chants and drumbeats ceased, and were replaced by shouts – one might say *complaints* – from the Sedgecombe supporters.

'Come *on*, Shuttles!' whined an impatient voice.

The *Shabab* boys were so surprised to find themselves in an attacking position that Khalid had to remind everyone of their duties.

'Ali!' he called. 'You take!'

Of course, thought Ali, and trotted over to the corner spot with a shake of his head.

Yunus was charged with the task of minding Jake on the halfway line.

For their part, the Sedgecombe team and supporters viewed the corner as a minor irritation: an unwelcome delay to their pursuit of a winning goal.

Which is why, when Ali whipped in a wicked, swerving cross, the Shuttles boys were focused only on meeting that cross and heading it clear.

It had not occurred to any of them that a *Shabab* head might get to that ball first.

Especially not the head of little Faris.

Will steadied himself, just a few feet from the near post, and prepared to head the ball away. But before he could do so the diminutive figure of Faris raced across in front of him and propelled himself upward.

Suspended momentarily in mid-air, he flicked his head up at the ball and sent a looping header over Will, over the Shuttles goalkeeper, and rippling into the far corner of the net.

'*David has slain Goliath!*' screamed Mr Bateman amid an explosion of noise from the *Shabab* contingent. Even Imam Munieb was jumping up and down now, punching the air with his familiar cry of '*mashallah!*'

Saleem's parents rose to their feet in applause and looked across at their oldest son, whose face was buried in his hands. When he looked up, it was toward the heavens.

The urgency with which Sedgecombe Shuttles attempted to respond only hindered their attacking play, and their crisp, clever passing all but vanished. When an over-hit pass sped away from Jake, Junayd saw his friend heave a huge, despondent sigh, and in that moment he knew there would only be one winner.

The final whistle blew to a mixture of delighted cries, disappointed groans, and gentle applause.

'Come on brothers,' urged Khalid. 'Shake hands and show some class.'

The full *Shabab* squad – for Junayd and Ibrahim had limped onto the pitch as well – sought out their defeated opponents and congratulated them on a fine performance.

And as they did so, the Sedgecombe support stirred into life once more. But this time it was not their own team to whom they showed their appreciation.

'*Three cheers for the* Shabab *team!*' rasped a hoarse voice. '*Hip hip ...*'

'*HOORAY!*'

'I'm not sure how you lost that,' said Junayd to Jake, extending his hand.

'I'm not sure either,' replied his friend as he shook the hand and wandered away.

'*Qadrullah* little bruv,' murmured Saleem, wrapping his arm around Junayd. 'It was written. Hard work too though, wasn't it?'

Junayd looked around at his exhausted teammates, and winced as he rubbed his leg.

'You can say that again.'

15. Victory

'Dear brothers and sisters,' smiled Imam Munieb. '*As-salamu 'alaikum wa rahmatullahi wa barakatuhu.*'

'*Wa 'alaikum as-salamu wa rahmatullahi wa barakatuhu,*' replied the gathered parents and boys, seated in rows of chairs before the Imam. Alongside them, in the comfiest chairs the mosque possessed, sat Mr Bateman and his wife: the guests of honour.

'*Alhamdulillah*, all praise is due to Allah, the Lord of the Worlds, the Beneficent, the Merciful, Master of the Day of Judgment. We ask Allah the Almighty to send His Peace and Blessings upon His Prophet Muhammad, *sallallahu alayhi wa salam*, and upon his family, and those who follow him until the Day of Standing, *Ameen.*'

The Imam went on, 'I am delighted that so many of you have come today to find out what your children have been learning about during our Sunday madrasa. As we see their development as Muslims I want all of us – including myself – to think about the road we are travelling along.

'Seeking knowledge is a *must*, and we can never stop looking for it. The day we think we have learned all there is that is worth knowing, we actually must have learned *nothing* at all. Didn't Allah the Almighty show the Prophet Musa, *alayhi salam*, that even when he thought he knew best of all people, there was somebody who knew better?

'You *will* see today, *inshallah*, that your children have learned a lot, and we pray to Allah *subhanahu wa ta'ala* that He benefits them with what they have learned of His Knowledge. What we have tried to do in the last two months has been about your children's learning, but I must tell you that nobody in this room has learned more over these months than I have.

'I have learned in a *real* way the importance of balance in life; of finding ways to help our children succeed. Not just making them accept the ways we know, when they may not be appropriate.

'I have learned that we can do more for young people if we trust them, and help them to meet the responsibilities we give them. More so than if we get angry with them and say that they do not deserve our trust in the first place.

'Today our presentation to you offers a look at what our future could be, *inshallah*, if we trust and support our children.'

Imam Munieb's boys recited from the Qur'an, and Salamah's girls explained some of the meanings of the holy book. After that several of the young Muslims stood to read biographies that they had prepared about the great young *sahabah,* the companions of the Prophet Muhammad: Abdullah ibn Abbas, Usama bin Zayd, and Aisha bint Abu Bakr. The boys and girls then had a mixed gender debate about whether: *'The young sahabah made an indispensible contribution to the dissemination of Islamic knowledge.'*

'This debate,' announced Abdullah, who had been selected to chair the proceedings, 'was instigated by Uncle

'Uthman, who has decided he would like to be involved in our lessons about the *sahabah*. *Jazakallah khayran*, Uncle, and we welcome any other ideas and support from the adults in our community.'

Among the parents in attendance was Adam's father, who had sought out Imam Munieb earlier to apologise for his manner a few weeks before.

'Adam was very upset not to be involved,' he admitted, 'and I couldn't help feeling afterwards that I was wrong to make him go to madrasa but not to let him play football. Anyway, I should not have spoken to you the way I did.'

'*Laa ba's*,' the Imam reassured him. 'A few weeks earlier I would have been telling myself I am mad!'

Adam's father smiled. 'No, my brother,' he insisted. '*You* are the sane one and, *mashallah*, the one who Allah has guided to a good deed. You saw an opportunity and grasped it, with Allah's help. We should all look at the good that has come from this and ask ourselves what *we* can also do for our community.'

He paused for a moment, and a quizzical smile formed upon his lips.

'You know what surprised me most of all, though,' he said. 'I didn't think you even liked football!'

Imam Munieb stroked his beard, his eyes twinkling.

'I didn't!' he grinned.

The morning ended with an awards ceremony to the football team. Each *Shabab* player was presented with the medal he had won by a member of the 'B' team.

Mr Miah was quietly thrilled to see Junayd receive his award, but even happier to hear Khalid's short speech.

'*As-salamu 'alaykum,*' began the *Shabab* captain. 'I know everyone thinks I talk too much, but I'm going to keep this short. *Alhamdulillah*, we won! We *did* play well, we *did* deserve it, we *did* fight for each other like brothers should, but Allah knows it was a miracle. And we thank Allah for our coach, Brother Saleem, because we couldn't have done it without him. Please can we all give him a big round of app ...'

'*Takbir!*' cried Imam Munieb, who always preferred to offer praise in the traditional manner.

'*Allahu akbar!*' came the rejoinder.

'*Takbir!*'

'*Allahu akbar!*'

'*Takbir!*'

'*ALLAHU AKBAR!*'

Glossary

Ahsanta (Arabic) *You have done well.*

Alhamdulillah (Arabic) *All praise is due to Allah.*

Allahu akbar (Arabic) *Allah is The Greatest.*

Ameen (Arabic) *Declaration of affirmation.*

As-salamu 'alaykum (wa rahmatullahi wa barakatuh) (Arabic) *May peace be upon you (and Allah's Mercy, and His Blessings).*

Baba (Arabic) *Dad.*

Barakah (Arabic) *Blessing (of Allah)/gift bestowed by God.*

Bismillah (Arabic) *In the name of Allah.*

Dadi (Sylheti) *Paternal grandmother.*

Deen (Arabic) *Religion/way of life grounded in one's religion.*

Fa-sabbih bi-hamdi rabbika wa'staghfir (Holy Qur'an)
Part of the final verse of Chapter 110 of the Holy Qur'an.
An approximate translation of its meaning is: Extol thy Sustainer's
Limitless Glory, and praise Him, and seek His Forgiveness.

Ya habibti (Arabic) *O' darling/beloved one.*

Halal (Arabic) *Permissible.*

Heshe kita khorray (Sylheti) *What are you doing later?*

Ho qutah (Sylheti) *That dog.*

Innahu kana tawwaba (Holy Qur'an) *The last part of the final*
verse of Chapter 110 of the Holy Qur'an. An approximate translation
of its meaning is: He (Allah) is ever An Acceptor of Repentance.

Jazakallah khayran (Arabic) *May Allah reward you with good.*

Jum'ah (Arabic) *Friday prayer.*

Khutbah (Arabic) *Sermon.*

Kita khorsot (Sylheti) *What have you done?*

Kita khoss (Sylheti) *What did you say?*

La ba's (Arabic) *No problem.*

Madrasa (Arabic) *School.*

Mashallah (Arabic) *Allah has willed it to be so.*

Min fadlik (Arabic) *Please (from your kindness).*

O bydee ai (Sylheti) *Come here.*

Qadrullah (Arabic) *Predestination of Allah.*

Sahabah *Followers of the Prophet Muhammad who had personal contact with him.*

Sallallahu 'alayhi wa sallam (Arabic) *Peace and blessings of Allah be upon him (said after mention is made of the Prophet Muhammad).*

Shaaree (Sylheti) *Sari – a long, thin piece of material worn as a dress by females from certain Asian countries.*

Shabab (Arabic) *Young people.*

Shukran jazeelan (Arabic) *Thank you very much.*

Shunna (Sylheti) *Gold. (Can be used as a term of affection, but here the word is used as an established call name – that of Saleem and Junayd's mother).*

Subhanahu wa ta'ala (Arabic) *Glorified and Exalted Be He (Allah).*

Subhanallah (Arabic) *Glory be to Allah.*

Surah al-Nasr (Holy Qur'an) *Chapter 110 of the Holy Qur'an. An approximate translation of the chapter's title is: The Victory.*

Tafaddal (Arabic) *Please, go ahead.*

Takbir (Arabic) *The name given to the expression 'Allahu akbar'.*

Ubba (Sylheti) *Father.*

Umma (Sylheti) *Mother.*

Wa 'alaykum as-salam (Arabic) *And upon you be peace.*

Ya Allah (Arabic) *O Allah (when supplicating to God).*

Acknowledgements

My deep appreciation to Shahina, for both your enthusiasm and your criticism … but above all, for allowing me to hole up in my room for hours on end. To Muhammad, for your encouragement and honest feedback on everything I've written. With thanks to Sr. Fatima for your input, and to Yosef for your positivity and drive down the home straight. *Jazakallah khayran* to you all. Last but not least, a special mention for Humayun, Naim, Karam, Rohullah, Yezen, Maruf, Omer, Karl, Jehan, Taariq, Yusif, Zak, Hisham, David, Houssam, Bishr, Riley, Bakr and Muhammad. You won't find yourselves in the story, but your influence is on every page.